I'm 16, I'm a witch, and I *still* have to go to school?

Hiccups are hiccups, right? Wrong! Aunt Hilda's hiccups may be the end of me *and* Western civilization if I can't find a cure for her magical/medical disorder. She accidentally yanked Benjamin Franklin into the 20th century, and now *I* have to figure out how to get him back where he belongs. And that's only part of the problem. . . .

My name's Sabrina and I'm sixteen. I always knew I was different, but I thought it was just because I lived with my strange aunts, Zelda and Hilda, while my divorced parents bounced around the world. Dad's in the foreign service. The *very* foreign service. He's a witch—and so am I.

I can't run to Mom—but *not* because she's currently on an archaeological dig in Peru. She's a mortal. If I set eyes on her in the next two years, she'll turn into a ball of wax. So for now, I'm stuck with my aunts. They're hanging around to show me everything I need to know about this witch business. They say all I have to do is concentrate and point. And I thought fitting in was tough!

You probably think I have superpowers. Think again! I can't turn back time and I'm on my own when it comes to love. Of course, there are some pretty neat things I *can* do—but that's where the trouble *always* begins. . . .

Sabrina, the Teenage Witch™ books

#1 Sabrina, the Teenage Witch
#2 Showdown at the Mall
#3 Good Switch, Bad Switch
#4 Halloween Havoc
#5 Santa's Little Helper
#6 Ben There, Done That

Available from ARCHWAY Paperbacks

Sabrina
The Teenage Witch™

Ben There, Done That

Joseph Locke

AN ARCHWAY PAPERBACK
Published by POCKET BOOKS
New York London Toronto Sydney Tokyo Singapore

This book is a work of fiction. Names, characters, places and incidents are products of the author's imagination or are used fictitiously. Any resemblance to actual events or locales or persons living or dead is entirely coincidental.

AN ARCHWAY PAPERBACK *Original*

An Archway Paperback published by
POCKET BOOKS, a division of Simon & Schuster Inc.
1230 Avenue of the Americas, New York, NY 10020

Copyright © 1998 by Viacom Productions, Inc. All rights reserved.

ISBN: 0-671-01680-6

First Archway Paperback printing January 1998

10 9 8 7 6 5 4 3 2 1

AN ARCHWAY PAPERBACK and colophon are registered trademarks of Simon & Schuster Inc.

SABRINA THE TEENAGE WITCH and all related titles, logos, and characters are trademarks of Archie Comics Publications, Inc.

Printed in the U.S.A.

IL 5+

For
Angela De La Cruz

Ben There, Done That

Chapter 1

When Hilda and Zelda Spellman walked into the living room in their robes, their jaws dropped and they stared in horror at the mess.

Salem, their black cat, stepped around them, hopped onto the back of the sofa, and looked around with apparent disinterest.

"There was an earthquake," Zelda said. "During the night, there was an earthquake, and we slept through it. That's the only thing that could make such a mess."

"I don't know," Salem said, settling down comfortably on the back of the sofa. "I once knew a couple of Siamese who were left alone in a house for a couple hours. What they did made this look like Martha Stewart's place."

Neither an earthquake nor Siamese cats were

to blame, of course. The disaster that had occurred in the house had been nothing more than the Annual Witches' May Eve party. The May Eve party was held on the last night of April every year, to ring in Beltane, the first of May, a celebration of spring and renewal. It had been Hilda's and Zelda's turn to host the May Eve party, so everyone had come to their house the night before.

"Who's going to clean this up?" Zelda asked as she and her sister made their way across the room.

"We're witches," Hilda said weakly as they both flopped onto the sofa. "We can clean it up in the blink of an eye."

Zelda let her head drop backward as she said, "I don't have the energy to blink an eye."

"That's nothing," Hilda grumbled. "I haven't even managed to open mine all the way yet."

"Well, it was a great party, Hilda . . . even if it *did* go too late."

"Late? You mean *early*. Chickens were sitting down to *brunch* when we went to bed."

"Maybe so, but we pulled it off," Zelda said, staring up at the ceiling as she slumped on the sofa. "I think it was a successful May Eve party. One they'll remember."

"Are you kidding? *I* barely remember it."

"Well, that's only because you had too much of Uncle Ruprecht's Venusian mead. I mean, there was plenty of *regular* mead available, but no . . . you had to have the *Venusian* stuff."

"Oh, please," Hilda said snidely. "That stuff is awful. The Venusians have *never* been able to make decent mead. It's always some ugly yellowish color. And their *cheese,*" she sneered. "It tastes like laundry lint."

"Well, Hilda, dear, you certainly didn't think Venusian mead was ugly last night."

Hilda frowned and turned her head slowly to her sister. "I . . . I didn't?"

"Are you *kidding?* You had so much of it last night, you were starting to *speak* Venusian!"

"You're not serious," Hilda said quietly, a look of dread growing on her face.

"I *am* serious. So, if you're feeling sick, don't complain to me." Zelda leaned forward with a sigh and massaged her stiff neck with her right hand, groaning slightly. "I've told you before, you're *allergic* to the stuff. You should avoid it like the plague, I said, but *no . . .* you went ahead and guzzled it like Gatorade."

Hilda frowned, blinking her eyes several times. "I had a lot of—er, well, *some* Venusian mead last night?"

"No. Not some. A *lot* of."

"Oh. Well . . . oh, dear . . . oh, my goodness."

"Yes, oh, dear, but your goodness had nothing to do with it," Zelda said sarcastically. "Remember what happened the *last* time Uncle Ruprecht dropped by with some of his Venusian mead?"

Hilda winced.

"You changed colors so many times in the next

3

month, we nearly went broke trying to keep up with your *wardrobe* needs!"

"Yes, I remember," Hilda said, rubbing her eyes. "I was plaid for a while . . . didn't leave the house for four days."

"Well, the plaid would've worked with a kilt and a set of bagpipes," Zelda said with a huffy tone. "But you were *puce* for a week, and we couldn't do a *thing* with you!"

Hilda leaned forward, put her elbows on her knees, and buried her face in her hands, sighing heavily.

"Oooh, no you don't," Zelda said, standing as she continued to massage her neck. "No sighing from you. You've made your bed, now lie in it. You're just going to have to grin and bear it, because we've got to go to the Beltane ceremony, and it starts in just an hour." Zelda frowned as she looked down at the floor. "How did the electric can opener get in here?"

"Look, Zelda, I really don't know if I can make it," Hilda said, her voice muffled as she spoke into the palms of her hands.

"Don't *even* start with me, Hilda. It's *Beltane!* The Maypole! The ribbons that represent our wishes, all being intertwined around the pole."

"My *brain* is intertwined around a pole," Hilda groaned.

"You *have* to go! And as you know, dear, there's a fine if you *don't* go. So, let's just get ourselves together here, okay? We can have some coffee, and"—Zelda propped her hands on her hips, looking around at the messy room—"we should clean up this eyesore before Sabrina comes downstairs. It's shameful and atrocious."

"*You* clean up the mess," Hilda said. "I'll make the coffee."

"Oh, all right," Zelda said with a sigh. She waved a hand through the air and muttered a spell.

The mess was gone in an instant. The living room was suddenly neat as a pin.

With both hands still pressed to her face, Hilda wiggled her index finger and made a noise in her throat. "Okay," she muttered. "Coffee's ready."

When Sabrina walked into the kitchen in her robe, Hilda and Zelda were just sitting down at the table with their cups of coffee. Once seated, Hilda's head drooped very low and her eyes were almost completely closed. But Zelda sat up straight and smiled at her niece.

"Good morning," Sabrina said cheerfully.

"Good morning, Sabrina," Zelda said, forcing herself to smile in spite of her weariness. "What would you like for breakfast?"

"Oh, no conjuring necessary, Aunt Zelda," Sabrina said. "I'm just gonna have a bowl of cereal the old-fashioned way." She went to the cupboard, removed a box, a bowl, and poured.

"G'morning, S'brina," Hilda muttered, her face just inches from her cup.

Sabrina froze for a moment, looked at Hilda, and frowned slightly, then glanced inquisitively at Zelda.

"Your aunt Hilda's not feeling very well," Zelda said. "We didn't get much sleep, so we're both kind of off center, if you know what I mean."

"How did the May Eve party go?" Sabrina asked as she opened the refrigerator. She removed a carton of milk and poured some over her cereal.

"It went beautifully," Zelda said. "It was a *big* success. And obviously, so was the silence spell we put around your bedroom so you could sleep." She lifted her mug and sipped her coffee. "Eeewww," she blurted, her entire face curling into a grimace of disapproval. "You call this *coffee?*" she asked, looking across the table at her sister. "It's weak as brown water!"

"Hey," Hilda said wearily, "I only had enough strength to use one finger . . . so sue me, okay?" She put her elbows on the tabletop and covered her face with both hands.

Zelda frowned at her sister, then passed a hand over her cup of coffee, her lips forming a brief, breathy spell. She sipped it again and nodded with approval. "That's better," she said. Turning to Sabrina again, she said, "I'm *so* sorry you won't be able to come to the Beltane festivities."

Sabrina poured herself a glass of orange juice and moved to the table. "I know, Aunt Zelda,"

Sabrina said, sitting down. "I wish I could go, too. But I've got school."

"Yes, and that's the only excuse the Witch Council will accept." She turned to Hilda and raised her voice slightly as she said, "Did you *hear* that, Miss Venusian mead? School is the *only* excuse they accept." Then she turned to Sabrina again, smiling. "But don't worry, dear. Next year, Beltane falls on a Friday. You won't have to worry about school, and you'll be able to attend both the May Eve party *and* the Beltane festivities."

Sabrina smiled at Zelda, then looked at Hilda. "Yeah, but for now . . . I'm worried about *her.*"

"Oh, don't worry about her," Zelda said quickly. "She'll be fine. Really. She just needs a little more time to wake up, that's all."

Salem hopped up on the table.

"Good morning, Salem," Sabrina said.

The cat did not respond. Instead, he crept over to Sabrina's bowl and cautiously leaned his head forward to sniff the cereal.

"Hey, get your face out of my cornflakes!" she said, giving him a nudge away from the bowl. "Get your own, nosey."

Salem stepped back and sat on his haunches. "But no one will buy the kind I like."

"I told you, Salem," Zelda said, "I will not get you a box of Lizard Flakes."

A spoonful of cornflakes stopped halfway to Sabrina's mouth as she screwed up her face and said, "Eeewww."

"It's *such* a waste," Zelda went on, "when we've got plenty of perfectly good lizards in the pantry to make our own."

"But you never *make* me any," Salem said despondently.

Zelda's eyebrows rose a notch as she looked at the cat with surprise. "Are you *kidding?* Salem, do you know how long it takes to flake a lizard?"

Giving up, Salem turned and walked slowly to the end of the table. "Besides," he said with a glance back at Zelda, "the boxes always had *prizes* in them." Then he hopped off the table. Voice fading as he left the kitchen, he said, "I found a little cellophane-wrapped chicken liver in one box."

Zelda took another sip of her coffee, then stood. "Well, Sabrina, you finish your breakfast."

"After that little exchange," Sabrina muttered, "I'm not sure I *can.*"

"Your aunt Hilda and I have to get ready for the Beltane ceremonies." With a wave of her arm and a brief flash of light, Zelda's robe and slippers were gone. They were replaced by a flowing red robe with silky folds that glimmered with flecks of gold.

Still sitting at the table with her face in her hands, Hilda was wearing a robe similar to Zelda's, but it was white.

"Those are beautiful!" Sabrina said, standing. She took her cereal bowl to the counter and drained her glass of orange juice with a few swallows.

"Thank you, Sabrina," Zelda said. "I designed them myself."

"Well, I'm gonna go upstairs and get ready for school," Sabrina said. "I haven't decided what I'm going to wear yet."

"Have a good day," Zelda said.

Hilda muttered something into her palms.

On her way out, Sabrina said, "I hope you feel better soon, Aunt Hilda."

As soon as Sabrina was gone, Hilda raised her head and said, "Okay, get this thing off me. I can't go."

"But it's *Beltane,* Hilda, you *have* to go! You'll be fined if you don't!"

Hilda looked up at her sister with heavy-lidded eyes. "I'll pay the fine. With interest. Just put me back in my robe and slippers so I can go back to bed."

Zelda released a long, disapproving sigh. "Hilda, what am I going to tell everyone? What am I going to tell *Drell?"*

Hilda was rocked by a violent hiccup. It caught her off guard and nearly knocked her out of her chair. "There, tell him *that.* Tell him I'd just hiccup my way around the Maypole and spoil everyone's rhythm." She stood slowly, a bit unsteadily, and reached over her shoulder to scratch her back. "Now, can I lose this dress, please? The tag is starting to make me itch."

"On one condition," Zelda said, holding up a

rigid forefinger. "You go *straight* to bed and rest, and I come back in two hours to check on you. If you're feeling better, you get dressed and go to the Other Realm with me."

"Okay," Hilda replied, rolling her eyes. "But *only* if I'm feeling better."

"All right, then." Zelda waved her arm and in a brief sparkle, Hilda was in her robe and slippers again. "Straight to bed, Hilda. But if I win the door prize, and it's edible, I'm *not* sharing it with you."

A half hour later, Sabrina came downstairs, dressed and carrying her bookbag. She decided on one more glass of orange juice before leaving and went to the kitchen. Pulling the carton from the refrigerator, she poured, then set the carton on the counter and drank, leaving the refrigerator door open. She closed her eyes as she tipped the glass back and finished it off in a few gulps. Putting the glass down with a satisfied sigh, Sabrina lifted the carton and turned to put it back in the refrigerator. She froze, letting out a startled yelp, and stared with wide eyes.

The refrigerator was gone. In its place stood a Holstein cow.

The cow lifted its head slightly and chewed its cud as it looked at Sabrina with big, stupid eyes. Sabrina jumped back when the cow mooed at her loudly. Then the cow continued chewing its cud, staring at the microwave oven.

Putting the carton on the counter, Sabrina

took in a breath to yell for her aunts, when she remembered they'd gone to the Beltane ceremonies. Instead, she shouted, "Saaaa-lem!"

As if from nowhere, the cat hopped up onto the island and stared at the cow.

"Well," Salem said, "there's little chance of running out of milk now."

"Yeah, b-but," Sabrina stammered, "now we don't have anything to keep it *cold* in!"

"Oh, don't worry." Salem ran his tongue from one side of his mouth to the other and back, purring loudly. "I'll drink it all before it goes bad."

"Salem . . . our refrigerator just turned into a *cow!* Did you have anything to do with this?"

"Me? *Hah!* If I could do *that,*" he said, nodding toward the cow, "the cupboards in this kitchen would've been filled with boxes of Lizard Flakes *long* ago. Each with a free prize inside, of course."

Sabrina rolled her eyes. "Do you have any idea *why* this happened?"

Salem turned to her and twitched his whiskers. "You spend enough time in *this* house and pretty soon you stop asking things like '*why.*'"

"Well, what am I gonna *do?*" she asked, waving at the unconcerned cow. "I've gotta go to school, and Aunt Zelda and Aunt Hilda are in the Other Realm . . ."

"Hilda's upstairs in bed."

"Really? Well, would you do me a favor and go tell her the refrigerator just turned into a cow?"

"There's no chance of telling her anything. She conjured up some sleeping dust and she's up there snoring . . . and hiccuping. I don't know how she sleeps through those hiccups. They make her whole bed shake . . . like that little girl's bed in *The Exorcist.*"

"Oh. Well, at least her head's not spinning around," Sabrina said. "Last Halloween, she kept doing that just to gross me out."

"So, what are you going to do about the cow, Sabrina?"

"What do you mean?"

"Well . . . if you're gonna keep it in *here,* I sure don't want to hear any more snide remarks about my litterbox."

"Yeah," Sabrina muttered, scratching her head.

"Why don't you try using magic?"

Sabrina thought about it a moment, mumbled a spell, then pointed at the cow. There was a slight sparkle around the cow, but it made a sputtering sound and disappeared. She tried again, and the same thing happened.

"However this happened," Sabrina said, *"I* can't fix it. I guess I should take him out to the backyard."

With a quick sweep of her arm, Sabrina produced a handful of hay and held it in front of the cow's nose. The cow sniffed, then nibbled a bit with its lips. As it was about to take a bite, Sabrina pulled away and started walking backward toward the back door. The cow followed her, slowly but surely, trying to get a bite of that hay.

Salem sat on the island and watched the black-and-white spotted cow make its way through the kitchen. "I used to have a shower curtain that color," he said. Then he went about washing his face.

☆

Chapter 2

☆

In spite of the fact that the refrigerator had turned into a cow while Sabrina was drinking her orange juice that morning, the first half of her day at school rolled along quite typically, with no surprises . . . and no other farm animals. At least, it rolled along typically until lunchtime.

Harvey and Jenny were in line ahead of Sabrina, so they went to a table while she was still getting her lunch. Once she had everything she wanted on her tray—spaghetti, green beans, some applesauce, a roll, and a bottle of grape juice—Sabrina surreptitiously waved her hand over it. She silently cast the same spell she cast every time she ate cafeteria food—a spell that made it taste like *real* food.

As she carried her tray to the table where Harvey and Jenny were waiting for her, Sabrina had no idea that Aunt Hilda was thinking about her at home.

Having just woke from her sleep, Hilda turned to look at the clock on her bedstand. It was already noon, and Zelda had not yet come back to check on her. That was fine with Hilda because she *still* didn't feel like going to the Other Realm to celebrate *anything,* let alone Beltane. She was just too drained of energy to go out, and she still had the blasted hiccups.

It occurred to Hilda that Sabrina was probably at lunch at that very moment. She hoped her niece was having a good day and that she got some decent food in that cafeteria. And as that thought occurred to her, Hilda shook the bed with another raucous hiccup.

At the very instant that Hilda hiccuped, Sabrina was leaning forward to put her lunch tray on the table, when something happened that made her freeze. The plastic cafeteria tray carrying her lunch turned into a sterling silver tray with a raised rose border; on the tray was pheasant under glass, wild rice, tender asparagus, fresh rolls, a bowl of hot soup, and a fruit cup. It was suddenly much heavier than the cafeteria tray and Sabrina stumbled forward, clanking the tray onto the table.

She stared dumbly at the tray for a moment, then looked at her friends. They were staring at her with mouths open.

Sabrina grinned, sat down beside Harvey, and said to him, with a haughty British accent, "Drive the car around front of the estate, Maximillian . . . I shall want to go to the country club directly after lunch."

They didn't laugh. They didn't even smile. They just stared at the extravagant, delicious-smelling food.

Sabrina laughed nervously. "C'mon, guys, it was a little joke."

After a moment, Harvey frowned and asked, "What kind of bird *is* that?"

"It's a pheasant," Sabrina said, brightening with an idea. "And there's enough for all of us. It was a surprise. Something my aunts just, uh . . . conjured up." She laughed again, more confidently this time.

"A surprise?" Jenny asked.

"Yeah. You know how my aunts are." Sabrina began cutting up the bird. "They just, y'know . . . dropped it into my hands a couple minutes ago."

"That was awfully nice of them," Harvey said as Sabrina dropped a slice of pheasant onto his tray.

They shared the beautifully prepared food on the silver tray and talked between bites. But Sabrina had a difficult time keeping up with the conversation.

What is going on, here? she kept asking herself.

Sabrina had grown accustomed to odd things happening around her ever since she'd learned, on her sixteenth birthday, that she was a witch from a whole family of witches. But all those strange occurrences—like having a talking cat, for example—happened for a reason. In one crazy way or another, everything that went on in their house made some kind of sense.

That morning, the refrigerator had turned into a cow for no reason Sabrina could imagine; even Salem had been puzzled. And when her cafeteria lunch had turned into the chef's special from a five-star restaurant . . . well, there was *certainly* no sense in *that!* Neither Aunt Zelda nor Aunt Hilda would ever disrupt Sabrina's day at school, especially in a way that would raise questions . . . like pheasant under glass in the school cafeteria, for crying out loud! Sabrina knew they would never do that . . . not *intentionally*. And if it wasn't intentional . . .

. . . then something was wrong. Had some other witch cast a bad spell on their family? But who would do such a thing? And why? Whatever it was, Sabrina couldn't stop thinking about it.

Her thoughts were interrupted by the sound of Libby's snooty voice as she approached their table. As usual, her two friends Cee Cee and Jill were just a couple steps behind her. Libby held an open bottle of grape juice in her hand . . . therefore, so did Cee Cee and Jill.

"Having a garage sale, huh?" Libby asked, looking down at Jenny.

Startled to be addressed by Libby, Jenny dropped her fork onto her tray and looked up at

Libby. "Uh, yeah. It's, um, y'know . . . something we do a couple times a year. My mom cleans out the closets and sells everything we don't want. She always has free balloons for the kids, and we—"

"When did you put that notice on the bulletin board?" Libby asked, leaning toward Jenny slightly.

"Notice?" Jenny blurted. "You mean about the garage sale?"

"What *else* are we talking about here?"

"I put that up this morning. I-I've done it before, and no one's ever complained."

"Maybe because when you put it up *before,* you were more careful about *where* you put it," Libby said, leaning forward even more as she lowered her voice.

Jenny blinked as she tossed a confused glance at Sabrina and Harvey.

"What's the matter, Libby?" Sabrina asked. "Did Jenny cover the daily soap opera update?"

Without laughing at Sabrina's remark, Jenny covered her open mouth as she looked up at Libby with feigned regret. "Oh, I'm sorry . . . did I cover up the cheerleading schedule?"

Libby sighed heavily and rolled her eyes. "You put your pathetic garage sale notice over my *poster.*"

"That was a *poster?*" Jenny asked, surprised. "I thought it was an emergency exits map."

"That," Libby snapped, "is an overhead photograph of my house during my spring swim

party last year. And the poster was there to announce *this* year's spring swim party. But instead of a picture of my house, all anyone can see is a list of the contents of your *garage.*"

"I'm sorry, Libby," Jenny said. "I didn't realize I'd—"

"Don't worry. I've already *removed* it. Post it someplace else next time." Libby released a sharp explusion of breath as she shook her head pathetically at Jenny.

"Wait a second," Jenny said, firmly now, as she backed her chair away from the table. "What's so wrong with a garage—" Jenny interrupted herself with a loud gasp of surprise as she shot out of the chair.

Libby stood staring at Jenny, mouth open, the bottle of grape juice in her hand tilted to one side and half empty. She'd spilled half of the grape juice all over Jenny. Libby's mouth snapped shut.

"I didn't mean to do that," she said.

"Hah!" Jenny blurted. "Didn't mean to do it. Tell me another one! I *said* I was sorry for covering your poster, so why'd you—"

"If you hadn't moved back so fast, I wouldn't've—"

"You would've done it *anyway*, Libby, admit it."

Libby's back stiffened and she leveled an icy stare at Jenny. "All right, then, *fine*. What difference does it make? That shirt you're wearing *belongs* in a garage sale!"

As Libby spun around, Cee Cee and Jill stepped aside to let her pass between them. The girls shot a couple haughty glances at Jenny, then fell into step behind Libby, marching like the good little soldiers they were.

Jenny winced as she sat down again, reaching behind her to peel her wet shirt from her back. "I can't believe she did that," Jenny grumbled.

"It was an accident," Harvey said before taking a bite of a hot roll.

"You have *got* to be joking," Jenny said, giving him a deadpan stare across the table.

"Why would she do that on purpose?" he asked, frowning. "That would be . . . well, it wouldn't be nice."

"Nice? Wait a second . . . are we talking about the same *person*, Harvey?"

He nodded. "Yeah, Libby. Right?"

"And you can use the word *nice* in reference to *Libby?*" Jenny asked, amazed.

"Come on, guys," Sabrina said uncomfortably. "You're letting this delicious lunch get cold."

They ate, but they did not stop talking. Harvey claimed Libby had always been nice to him, and Jenny claimed Libby had *never* been nice to her, or to *anyone*. Harvey thought Libby had spilled the grape juice accidentally, maybe bumped by Jenny's chair when she scooted it away from the table; Jenny, of course, insisted the grape juice had been spilled intentionally. It went on and on, until Jenny turned to Sabrina and said, "Would you please try to communicate with this alien life form? I mean, can you *believe* what he's saying?"

Sabrina didn't want to get involved, but she had no choice. "I'm afraid Libby's not often a very nice person, Harvey. In fact, I think even most of the people who *like* Libby would agree she's not a very nice person."

"See, Harvey?" Jenny said. "I'm *not* crazy. *Sabrina* saw Libby spill that grape juice on purpose, too."

Sabrina's attention was suddenly torn from her lunch. "Huh? What'd you say?"

"I'm just saying you saw Libby spill that grape juice on me intentionally, like I've been trying to tell Harvey here."

"Oh, no, Jenny," Sabrina said, shaking her head. "I didn't say that."

"You *didn't?*"

"I know she spilled it on you," Sabrina said, "but I don't know if it was on purpose."

Jenny's face pulled together into a frown. "But how can you *say* that, Sabrina?"

Sabrina shrugged. "I wasn't paying attention. Hey, this pheasant's pretty good, you know? I was eating, okay?" She turned to Harvey. "But it's the kind of thing Libby *would* do, Harv. You've been hanging around her long enough, you should know."

"But she's always been nice to *me*," Harvey insisted.

"That's because you're a *guy*," Jenny retorted.

"She's nice to Cee Cee and Jill, and *they're* not guys," Harvey countered.

"You call *that* nice? She treats them like dirt! They may not be guys, but they sure are *sheep.*"

It went on, and even began to escalate as Jenny and Harvey raised their voices. Finally, Sabrina stood and lifted the heavy silver tray with some effort. "Look, you guys," she said, "I can't digest my food if you're going to argue. I'll see you in American History class."

Ignoring the stares it got as she passed, Sabrina carried the silver tray to the window and slid it over the aluminum surface to Mr. Gurber, who stacked the trays on the other side. But he didn't move. Mr. Gurber just stared at the fancy silver tray and the remains of pheasant under glass. His bushy mustache didn't even twitch.

"Great lunch, Mr. Gurber," Sabrina said, smiling.

As Sabrina walked away, Mr. Gurber called over his shoulder, "Okay, who's the comedian?"

☆

Chapter 3

☆

In American History that day, Mrs. Hecht assigned a research paper. The paper was to be about any one of the men who signed the Declaration of Independence.

Sabrina wondered if even the most accomplished witch—for example, Drell, Head of the Witch Council—might be jealous of the chilling supernatural powers possessed by some teachers. Before Mrs. Hecht had uttered a word in class that day, Sabrina had known something was coming . . . a book report, an oral report, some kind of assignment. Sabrina had seen it in Mrs. Hecht's eyes, just as she'd seen it in the eyes of all her other teachers . . . that bright glimmer that comes with the realization that somewhere within the city limits, someone under the age of eighteen might have three or four minutes of spare time. Whenever Sabrina saw that look, she thought to herself, *Time for an assignment!*

Sabrina decided immediately to write a paper on Benjamin Franklin. The guy went kite-flying in electrical storms and wanted the turkey to be the national bird, for crying out loud . . . he *had* to be the goofiest of the forefathers and would, at least, keep her from getting bored while writing the paper.

As they left class, Sabrina and Jenny agreed to hit the library together after school.

It was at about that time Aunt Zelda returned from the Other Realm.

Hilda sat up in bed as Zelda walked into the room and began to pace. A cow mooed outside the window.

"Aren't you back a little early?" Hilda asked, one second before another hiccup made her jump.

"Oh, it was *awful,*" Zelda said, folding her arms tightly over her chest. "Absolutely *horrible!*"

"What was? What *happened?*"

"I don't know what happened yet. *Nobody* does!" Zelda added, throwing up her arms, then letting them slap at her sides. "Right in the middle of the ceremonies, the Maypole and everyone dancing around it turned into . . . in-to . . . a ring of little ponies wearing feather hats and just walking around and around in that same circle."

Hilda's gasp was interrupted by another hiccup. "You're *kidding!*" she blurted. "But who would *do* such a thing?"

Another long, doleful moo came from outside the window.

"No one!" Zelda said. "That's what makes it so *weird.* No one would disrupt Beltane that way intentionally . . . and it wasn't like a spell was being cast by someone, it was more like a . . . a . . . well, like weather. It just *happened."*

"That doesn't make any sense," Hilda said, frowning.

"Exactly," Zelda said, still pacing. "That's what's got everyone so confused. And Drell is a nervous *wreck.* The whole thing makes about as much sense as . . . as . . ."

The cow mooed again.

". . . as a cow in our backyard," Zelda said, pacing straight over to the window and opening the sash. "Hilda, *why* is there a cow in our backyard?"

"Is *that* what it is?" Hilda asked, rubbing her sleepy eyes. "I've been dozing all day . . . I thought the neighbors were just having a loud but very slow argument."

When Hilda hiccupped again, Zelda saw a brief shimmer of light in the neighbor's backyard, and a patio table with an umbrella and three plastic chairs disappeared. In the table's place stood another cow, staring at the ground without a hint of surprise.

The next moo was a duet.

"Uh-ooohhh!" Zelda exclaimed as realization struck her. She spun around and rushed to Hilda's bedside, saying, "You've *got* to stop hiccupping!"

"You're telling *me?"* Hilda said as she lay back down on the bed. "I've tried everything, and nothing works. I've been rattling the bed with these things all day." Another one struck her and, sure enough, the bed rattled.

"No!" Zelda cried. "I *mean* it, you have *got* to *stop!* Your hiccups are *doing* things!"

"Yes, they're making my eyes water."

"You just hiccupped a cow into the neighbor's backyard! Right in front of my eyes! I *saw* it! Now there are two cows out there!"

Hilda sat up again, but cautiously this time, a frown deepening as she rose. "What are you talking about, Zelda?"

"You've got something," Zelda said. "A witch bug." She pressed a hand to her heart and took a quick step backward. "Good *grief,* I hope it's not contagious!" She began pacing again.

"Don't be *silly,* Zelda, it's just a case of the *hiccups.* I've had them before. I'm fine."

Zelda stopped pacing suddenly, turned to Hilda and snapped her fingers as she exclaimed, "The *mead!* It's another reaction to the Venusian mead, Hilda! Last time, you changed colors, and this time you . . . you've got . . . runaway magic *hiccups."*

"Oh, no," Hilda whispered, giving her sister a

look of dread. "And I've been hiccupping all day long. What . . . have I been up to?"

"I don't know, but we don't have time to find out," Zelda said solemnly. "We've got to contact Dr. Leiderhosen."

"Dr. *Anton* Leiderhosen? Oh, he retired long ago."

"Not anymore. His retirement license was revoked. I've never been able to find out exactly *why* . . . it was all very mysterious. There's no doubt a delicious scandal behind the whole thing, but we don't have time for that now. I've got to reach him."

Hilda hiccupped again.

The sisters stared at one another with expressions of helpless fear.

What had *that* hiccup just done . . . and *where?*

Sabrina and Jenny left the library with all the books they needed on their chosen topics.

"I'd still rather write a paper on Betsy Ross," Jenny said as they headed home on foot.

"I told you, Jenny, she did *not* sign the Declaration of Independence."

"Yeah, but she did all that sewing! That should count for something, don't you think?"

"Thomas Jefferson is fine, Jenny."

As they walked, Jenny complained about Harvey's behavior at lunch.

"You're not still letting that bother you, are you?" Sabrina asked.

"Well, of *course!* Wouldn't you?" Jenny asked.

"You know Harvey didn't mean anything by what he said. He just sees things differently than we do."

"That's the *point,* Sabrina! How can he not see the way she treats us? Unless he just doesn't *care.* People never notice the things they don't care about."

Sabrina was genuinely surprised. She stopped walking and turned to Jenny. "You can't be serious. Harvey is one of your best *friends.*"

"I'm not sure I want that kind of friend. I mean, I've said some very personal things to you and Harvey, the kind of things people would only tell their friends. How do I know he's not off blabbing it all to Libby?"

"Jenny, Harvey would *never* do that! You know he's not a gossip. And he'd never do anything to hurt you."

"If he doesn't see the way Libby treats me, if he doesn't see how I feel about her . . . well, if he can't see how *she* hurts me, then what makes you think he'd give a second thought to hurting me himself? Which is why I don't intend to speak to him again."

Sabrina frowned. She realized that Jenny's feelings had been hurt . . . but she thought never speaking to Harvey again was taking it a bit too far.

"Look," Sabrina said, "I understand what

you're saying. I just think maybe you're making too big a deal out of it."

"Well, I don't understand what *you're* saying, Sabrina. I'm surprised you don't feel the same way I do. Harvey's your friend, too."

"I know, Jenny, and I think that's why it's so hard being in the middle of something like this."

"Oh," Jenny said, somewhat sadly. She started walking again, and Sabrina fell into step beside her. "I'm sorry, Sabrina. I didn't mean to trap you in the middle of this."

As they passed a house with a green fenced-in lawn, Sabrina started to respond, but instead, she stumbled to a halt with her jaw slack. There was a sofa in the front yard of that house. And it wasn't just *any* sofa . . . it was Aunt Zelda's and Aunt Hilda's sofa, the one from their living room! Sabrina recognized the pillows and Aunt Zelda's shawl draped over one arm. A little boy and girl were playing on the sofa like chattering monkeys.

Something really, *really* weird was going on . . . but Sabrina couldn't ignore her conversation to think about it right now.

"I-I-I know you didn't, Juh-Jenny," Sabrina stammered as she kept walking, fighting the urge to stand there gaping at the sofa, wondering what it was doing in someone's front yard. She hoped Jenny didn't notice it.

"Is something wrong?" Jenny asked.

"No, n-no, nothing, I'm fine. I just don't want you to feel like you owe me a sofa."

"What?"

"I mean, an *apology*. I know you didn't mean to—"

Jenny stopped walking and stared at Sabrina with a puzzled look and asked, "Did you just say I owe you a *sofa?*"

"No, no, no, an apology. You don't owe me an apology. I knew you didn't mean to put me on the spot, that's why I pointed it out. But I didn't take offense, because I know you well enough to know you wouldn't intentionally do anything like that. And that's what I'm hoping you'll do with Harvey. Just know he didn't mean to hurt you and then point it out to him that way. Nicely. But don't stop talking to him."

"Uh-uh . . . not this time. I want to make *sure* he gets the point."

"So you're gonna . . . what? Make him choose between the two of you? Your team or her team? Jenny, you and Harvey aren't in fourth grade anymore."

"What difference does that make? Friends are supposed to be forever. I want to make sure Harvey knows I'm hurt, and *why*. And I want him to figure it out on his own, so don't say anything to him about it. I promise not to put you on the spot, but it doesn't count if you do it yourself by poking your nose in."

When Jenny smiled at her, Sabrina knew she was serious. She always smiled that way when she made up her mind about something.

"Well, for the record," Sabrina said, tossing

one final glance over her shoulder at the children climbing on the sofa, "I think you're making a mistake. But I'll stay out of it."

They came to a corner and said good-bye as Jenny turned right down her street, and Sabrina walked on. Once she knew Jenny couldn't see her, Sabrina turned and looked back toward the house.

Whatever was going on, Sabrina had to let her aunts know immediately. She looked around quickly to make sure no one was paying any attention to her, then hunkered down behind a big blue public mailbox. With a simple waggle of some fingers, she disappeared in a multicolored sparkle—

—and appeared at home in the kitchen. She looked around for her aunts, but she was alone. She plopped her book bag onto the table, then left the kitchen and hurried upstairs.

"Why is our sofa in somebody's front yard halfway between here and the school?" Sabrina asked as she walked into Aunt Hilda's bedroom.

Aunt Hilda was lying in bed, and Aunt Zelda had been pacing when Sabrina came in. Now she stood frozen in mid-step, staring at her niece.

"Our sofa's in someone's yard?" Aunt Zelda asked after a long silence.

"Yes. There are children climbing on it," Sabrina added as Salem ambled into the room.

"With children, nobody ever complains," he said. "But a *cat* gets on the sofa, and you'd think somebody brought a cow into the house." He hopped up onto the foot of Hilda's bed and sat facing Sabrina. "You're home early, Sabrina. If you were smart, you wouldn't have come home at all."

"What?" Sabrina asked, wincing at the cat.

"In fact," Salem went on, sounding rather bored, "if I were you, I'd run for my life. Your aunt Hilda has a bad case of the hiccups. And not just *any* hiccups, either. *Witchups.* And boy, do they pack a punch!"

"I'm afraid it's true, Sabrina," Aunt Zelda said wearily. "Hilda seems to be having an allergic reaction to the Venusian mead she drank last night. Now, every time she hiccups, something magical happens. We've got a cow in our backyard, and the sofa turned into a swing set."

"That's not all," Sabrina said. "Our sofa's in somebody's front yard, and that cow in the backyard . . . that *used* to be our refrigerator." She told them about the silver tray and elaborate meal that had appeared in her arms at lunch in the cafeteria.

Frowning, Aunt Zelda said, "So . . . that means our refrigerator is standing out in a field with a bunch of cows somewhere?"

Sabrina nodded. "And someone at a *very* fancy restaurant got a school cafeteria meal." She sighed and shook her head, muttering, "They're lucky it wasn't Taco Tuesday."

"I'm sorry," Aunt Hilda said. There was a

slight whimper to her voice. "I . . . I didn't *mean* to do any of that."

Sabrina went to the bed and took her aunt's hand. "I know, Aunt Hilda. It wasn't your fault." She turned to Aunt Zelda and asked, "Isn't there something you can do for her? A spell? A potion?"

Aunt Zelda frowned thoughtfully for a moment. She waved both hands over Aunt Hilda, muttering a spell, then pointed down at her and finished loudly, ". . . and hiccups be *gone!*"

There was a brief sparkle around Aunt Hilda, but it sputtered out like a short in a circuit. Aunt Hilda hiccupped again.

"Same thing happened when I tried to get our refrigerator back," Sabrina said.

"Well," Aunt Zelda said, "a few minutes ago, I got on the horn and called Dr. Leiderhosen's office."

"Dr. *who?*" Sabrina asked.

"Oh, no, not him . . . ever since that stupid British TV series, he's too *good* to see patients. No, I mean Dr. Anton Leiderhosen, the most famous—"

"And infamous," Salem said under his breath.

"—witch doctor since Louis Pasteur."

Sabrina's face slowly scrunched up as she stared at Aunt Zelda. "Pasteur wasn't a witch doctor," she said.

"Of course not. But that didn't stop people from *calling* him a witch doctor." She giggled. "And oh, how he *hated* that!"

"What did the doctor say?" Sabrina asked.

"Oh, they're backed up at the office. The receptionist is supposed to call me back."

"Is there anything I can do for you, Aunt Hilda?" Sabrina asked.

"No, dear, but thank you for asking." She hiccupped again, looked around with a touch of panic in her eyes to see that nothing weird had happened, then relaxed. "How was your day, Sabrina?"

Sabrina's shoulders sagged as she released a heavy sigh. "I've had better."

"Something wrong?" Aunt Hilda asked.

Before Sabrina could reply, a phone booth appeared in the middle of the room, and a loud honking sound made Sabrina wince. Instead of a receiver, a curved, conelike horn was hanging from the chrome hook on the side of the long, rectangular black phone. The hornlike receiver was cordless.

"Ah, there's the horn now," Aunt Zelda said. "Excuse me while I get this," she said to Sabrina. She stepped into the booth, lifted the horn, and put it to her ear. "Hello?" she said quietly. "Yes, this is she. I called to make an appointment with Dr. Leiderhosen. It's for my sister, actually. She's got some kind of—" She paused, frowned. "Well, when will he be back?" Another pause. "Oh, we couldn't *possibly* wait that long! This is an *emergency!* Where *is* he?" She listened a moment. "The belt of *Orion?* Which notch? Well . . . like I said, this *is* an emergency. If you could just contact him and—" She stopped a moment, mouth open, then pressed her lips together and frowned. "One of his *students?* But that would be—" She stopped and rolled her eyes. "Hang on a second. Call waiting." She put the horn to her mouth, blew into it, and made a loud honking sound. Putting it back to her ear, she said, "Yes? . . . No, I do *not* want to buy a subscription to the *Witches' Chronicle!*" She blew into the horn again, put it to her ear, and said, "Sorry about that. Um, excuse me just a moment." Aunt Zelda stepped out of the booth, turned to Sabrina and Aunt Hilda, and said, "I'll take this in the hall, if you don't mind." She turned and left the room, speaking quietly into the horn.

Salem sat at the foot of Aunt Hilda's bed, purring as he bathed himself leisurely.

"Why did you have a bad day, dear?" Aunt Hilda asked, giving Sabrina's hand a squeeze. She hiccupped again and the bed squealed beneath its force.

"My two best friends are kind of having a fight over something," Sabrina said, "and I'm caught in the middle." She told Aunt Hilda about her lunch with Jenny and Harvey, about their disagreement over Libby's personality. "It's just so . . . *stupid.* But I think it really hurt Jenny's feelings, and that's why she's taking it so seriously. If she could just trade places with Harvey for an hour and see things the way *he* sees them, she'd know he didn't mean to hurt her. He'd *never* do that."

Aunt Hilda hiccupped loudly, then said, "Of course he wouldn't. Harvey's a very sweet boy. It's just that . . . well, sometimes he's a little narrow-sighted and doesn't see the big picture." She smiled.

Sabrina sighed. "You know, every one of us has a million opinions . . . but we've each got only one perspective. Somehow, it just doesn't seem fair."

Patting her niece's hand, Aunt Hilda said, "Oh, don't be silly, Sabrina. Fairness was outlawed *long* before the discovery of fire."

"I'd like to get together with them tonight and try to patch things up, but Mrs. Hecht assigned a paper today."

"Oh? What kind of paper do you have to write?"

"It's for American History. I stopped by the library and got a bunch of books on Benjamin Franklin."

Aunt Hilda hiccupped again, rocking the bed, then looked up at her niece for a long moment, her face darkening with guilt. "I'm sorry if I embarrassed you at lunch, Sabrina. Really, I didn't *mean* to."

"I know, Aunt Hilda. You couldn't help it . . . you're sick. Besides . . . by the end of lunch, Jenny and Harvey were so busy arguing about Libby, I think they'd *forgotten* about the pheasant under glass."

"I just happened to wake up at noon," Aunt Hilda said, "and I realized you'd be going to lunch. I wondered how your day was going, and hoped you'd get some decent food in that cafeteria. I had no *idea* that my hiccups would—"

"What did you say?" Sabrina asked, her eyes widening. "You . . . you *thought* about me? About my *lunch?* And . . . you *hiccupped* when you thought about me?"

"Well, yes, I suppose . . ."

At the foot of the bed, Salem had stopped bathing and was now paying attention to the conversation.

"What about the cow, Aunt Hilda? Do you remember thinking about a cow this morning?"

"Oh, I was asleep all morning. Until noon. But . . ." Aunt Hilda seemed to shrink beneath the bedcovers as she thought back, frowning. ". . . I did . . . *dream* about a cow."

"I'm not sure I want to know the answer to this question," Salem said, "but . . . did you also dream about a swing set?"

"No," Aunt Hilda whimpered. "But I . . . I did dream about . . . lounging on a sofa in the sun."

Sabrina and Salem exchanged a wide-eyed look of sudden realization.

Aunt Zelda came back into the room, saying, "Dr. Leiderhosen is at a conference in one of the notches of the belt of Orion, of all places, and he can't be reached. They're going to send one of his students to examine you, Hilda."

"A *student?*" Aunt Hilda said with a gasp. "Why, that . . . that's *insulting.*"

"That's what I thought," Aunt Zelda said, nodding. "But we'll just have to put up with the student for now. I'll talk to Drell and see if he can contact Dr. Leiderhosen. Of course, knowing Drell, he's probably off reversing volcanos in Peru . . . but at least I'll be able to *find* him."

"Aunt Zelda!" Sabrina blurted, clutching her arm. "I just figured out something about these hiccups!"

"You did? What? *What?*"

"Every time Aunt Hilda hiccups, something magical happens. But it's *not* random! The magic is influenced by whatever she happens to be thinking about at the moment she hiccups!"

"This is disastrous," Salem said nervously. "Absolutely catastrophic."

"Do you know what that means, Hilda?" Aunt Zelda asked, stepping over to her sister's bedside. "That means you *have* to stop *thinking!*"

"Oh," Salem said, cocking his head. "Maybe this'll be much easier than I thought!"

"Hey!" Hilda snapped, giving the cat a nudge with her foot beneath the covers.

"I know how we can turn off Hilda's thought processes!" Salem said excitedly. "Somebody slip a Pauly Shore movie into the VCR!"

Aunt Zelda propped a fist on her hip and glared at the cat with narrowing eyes. "Don't you have some rodents to chase, Salem?"

"Oh, all right," Salem whined, standing. He hopped off the bed and headed out of the room, saying, "When you finally realize what a brilliant idea it is . . . I'll be in the hall closet."

"Could I talk with you for a second?" Sabrina asked, taking Aunt Zelda's arm and leading her to the open bedroom doorway. In a breathy whisper, she said, "I have an idea."

"Good!" Aunt Zelda whispered. "We need all the help we can get."

"If you can't get Dr. Leiderhosen here right away, why don't we try a few *mortal* cures for the hiccups?"

Aunt Zelda's eyebrows shot upward excitedly. "Do you know any?"

"Well, I've heard a really good scare can stop the hiccups."

Aunt Zelda's eyebrows shot downward as she chewed on a thumbnail. "A good scare, huh? Hmm . . . let me see what I can do."

"Hey!" Aunt Hilda called. "You two are *whispering! That's not *fair!*"

"Fairness was outlawed before fire was discovered, remember?" Sabrina said with a smile, returning to the bedside with Aunt Zelda.

Without warning, Aunt Zelda transformed herself, in a cloud of sparkles, into Barney the dinosaur and said, in a goofy voice, "Let's all sing a song!"

Aunt Hilda covered her face with both hands and released a long, shrill, terrified scream.

Barney gave Sabrina a conspiratorial nod as Aunt Hilda continued to scream and scream, until—

—her screaming was interrupted by a violent hiccup. In the blink of an eye, Aunt Zelda was herself again, looking very disappointed.

Aunt Zelda sighed and said, "Well, obviously . . . *that* didn't work."

Salem trotted into the room, his eyes filled with panic. "What happened? What's wrong? What's going on?"

"We thought a good scare might stop Aunt Hilda's hiccups," Sabrina said to the cat. "So Aunt Zelda turned herself into Barney the dinosaur."

Salem gasped as he turned to Aunt Zelda with a look of horror. "Barney the *dinosaur?* Are you trying to scare her . . . or *kill* her?"

"It was a good try," Aunt Hilda said sadly. "I appreciate it."

Sabrina turned to Aunt Zelda and said, "Look, I'm gonna go downstairs, get my books, then change my clothes. There are more mortal cures for hiccups. We'll work on it, okay?"

"Don't let me get in the way of your homework, sweetie," Aunt Hilda said.

Sabrina smiled. "Don't worry, I won't. I'll be right back." Sabrina left the room and hurried downstairs.

In the kitchen, Sabrina's shoes squeaked on the tile floor as she jerked to a stop, staring up at the strange man, her mouth hanging open.

"Young lady," the man said, giving her a worried look, "where *am* I?"

He wasn't very tall, had a round belly and skinny legs. A wreath of long gray hair surrounded the shiny bald top of his head. He wore tiny round spectacles on his nose, and some *really* funky clothes.

Sabrina didn't have to ask who he was . . . she already knew.

Standing on the kitchen table, looking at Sabrina with an expression that suggested he'd just eaten some bad clams, was a befuddled Benjamin Franklin.

☆

Chapter 4

☆

Mr., uh . . . Franklin?" Sabrina asked nervously.

"Do I know you?" he asked, cocking his head.

"Oh, no, you don't. But I've seen your picture."

"Ah." He smiled. "Which one? One of the better renderings, I hope."

"Uh . . ." She smiled, chuckled uncomfortably, then said, "Would you please excuse me for a second?" Sabrina turned her back to him, cupped a hand to the side of her mouth, and shouted at the top of her lungs, "Aunt *Zeldaaa!*"

"Young lady," Franklin said. When Sabrina turned to face him again, he was still smiling.

"Would you be so good as to tell me where I am?"

"Oh, uh, well . . . this is, um . . . you're in, uh . . . the kitchen," she replied, grinning nervously.

Aunt Zelda hurried into the kitchen and said, "Sabrina, what in the world is—" She stumbled to a halt and gawked up at the man standing on the kitchen table. She slapped a hand to her chest and blurted, "Oh my goodness, it's Benjamin Franklin."

Sabrina pulled a chair out from the table and Franklin stepped down onto it, then down to the floor. He went over to Aunt Zelda, took her hand in his, and said, "At your service, madam." He bowed stiffly and brushed his lips over the back of her hand, saying as he stood, "And with pleasure."

Aunt Zelda's eyes saddened. "Oh, Benjie . . . don't tell me you don't *remember* me!"

Franklin's smile tilted, then drooped, and his eyebrows rose above his spectacles. "Remember you? Well, I . . . I must confess there is a certain familiarity . . ."

Zelda girlishly slapped his shoulder, startling him. "That time your coach broke down, and my sister and I put you and your friends up. Remember? We were having a party that night and the house was *full!*"

After blinking a few times, he nodded slightly. "Good heavens, yes, I *do* have a vague recollection of that. Very hospitable of you, madam," he said with a bow of his head.

"Your recollection is probably vague," Aunt Zelda said understandingly, "because my uncle Ruprecht was there and you had a couple glasses of his Venu—er, I mean, his homemade mead." She closed her eyes and laughed, shaking her head. "Your hair stood straight up on end and you spoke fluent Yiddish for about three hours, but that was all. You were very lucky and you should be grateful. By the way—how's your friend with those awful-smelling whalebone teeth?"

Uh-oh, Sabrina thought as she felt the situation getting out of hand. She looked at her book bag on the kitchen table. It had been bulging when she'd placed it there earlier, but now it looked deflated. When she looked in the bag, she saw that the books she'd brought home from the library were gone. Sabrina went to her aunt's side, her back to Franklin.

"Aunt Zelda," Sabrina whispered. "Aren't you wondering *why* he's here?"

"Your coach didn't break down again, did it, Benjie?" She poked him in the ribs playfully and he jumped a step back, giggling.

"Aunt Zelda," Sabrina whispered again. She gestured to her book bag on the table. "My *books* are gone. My *history* books." When Aunt Zelda stared blankly at her, Sabrina leaned forward, cupped her hand to her aunt's ear, and whispered, "My history books about *Benjamin Franklin!*"

Aunt Zelda's eyes widened. "Oh, you're *right!*" Looking at her watch, she said, "Good grief, what century is it?"

"It was Aunt Hilda's hiccups! My books are gone, but *he's* here!"

Aunt Zelda frowned. "Which means your books are . . ." She turned to Franklin again. "Tell me, Benjie . . . where were you before you came here?"

"B-b-but . . . I still don't know how I *got* here!" Franklin asked. "And what place *is* this?"

"Well, let's take one question at a time, okay?" Aunt Zelda said. "And I asked first. So . . . where were you just before you came here?"

"I was gathered with some like-thinking gentlemen and we were about to sign a document of *tremendous* import that will—"

"The Declaration . . . of Independence?" Sabrina asked warily.

Franklin's face brightened. "Why, yes!"

Sabrina exchanged a saucer-eyed glance with her aunt.

"But then," Franklin went on, "Jefferson and Hancock started playing keep-away with the blasted quill and the time was getting away from us, and we were trying to persuade them to be *serious* . . . and then . . . quite magically . . . I was *here.*" He shrugged, confused.

"Which means my books are *there,*" Sabrina whispered to Aunt Zelda. "Just like the sofa trading places with the swing set."

"Excuse us for just a moment," Aunt Zelda said to Franklin with a smile. She took Sabrina's elbow and led her from the kitchen into the dining room. She spoke in a panicky whisper when she said, "Sabrina, if your history books have traded places with Benjie, then . . . well, do you know what that *means?*"

Sabrina gave her aunt a cautious look. "That I'm gonna have to pay the library a heck of a late fine?"

"Oh, no it's *much* worse than that, it's . . . well, it could be *disastrous!*"

"What do you mean?"

"Well, the Witch Council absolutely *forbids* any interference in historical events! If your books are *there* with all those men who are about to sign the Declaration of Independence, they might *read* them . . . and what they read might influence their decisions! That would be catastrophic, Sabrina . . . and it would send the Witch Council into an absolute *tizzy!*"

"But I thought you said you already *know* Benjamin Franklin," Sabrina said, wincing with confusion. "You said you've *met!*"

"Yes, we did meet, and we had a *great* time," Aunt Zelda said with a wistful smile. "He may not look like much, but he's got a *wonderful* mind . . . and he's not a bad kisser, either!"

"Aunt Zelda, could we please stay on the subject?"

"Yes, of course, I'm sorry. I met him years ago. Over two hundred, in fact." She reached up and patted a hand to her hair a few times, primping for a moment. "Remember, Sabrina . . . I'm older than I look."

"Well, *obviously.*"

Aunt Zelda's hand dropped to her side and she became instantly serious. "Okay, we've got a serious problem on our hands. I'll just have to—"

She swallowed her words when they heard three beeps in the kitchen, then the microwave oven began to hum industriously. Franklin let out a loud, sharp yelp!

Sabrina and Aunt Zelda rushed into the kitchen to find Franklin pressing himself fearfully against the edge of the island, his hands pressed to the sides of his face as he gawked in horror at the rumbling microwave. Aunt Zelda reached over and turned it off.

"I am *terribly* sorry," he said. "I was simply . . . I had no idea what . . . I mean to say, I was only trying to—"

"Don't worry about it, Benjie," Aunt Zelda said. "No harm done." She went to his side, put an arm around his shoulders and began to lead him to the kitchen table, saying, "Would you do me a big favor and just take a seat here for a few minutes?" She stepped away from him and put her hands on the back of the chair Sabrina had pulled away from the table earlier. "Just sit down right here and relax for a few minutes. Would you mind?"

"Anything to please you, madam," Franklin said with a pleasant smile as he seated himself in the chair. Aunt Zelda stood at his side as he said, "But if I may just ask you one—"

Aunt Zelda held up a rigid forefinger. "Ah-ah-ah!" she interrupted. "No questions now. Save those for later. Just sit right here, okay, Benjie? My niece, Sabrina, and I have to step out of the room for just a few minutes. We'll be *right* back, so . . . don't move . . . and don't *touch* anything, okay?"

This time, Franklin's smile appeared forced as he nodded and said, "If that is your wish, madam, that is what I shall do."

Aunt Zelda patted the bald top of his head as she said, "Oh, thank you *so* much, Benjie. Be right back!" Turning to Sabrina, she said, "Upstairs."

They hurried out of the kitchen, leaving Benjamin Franklin—one of the fathers of the country—sitting at the kitchen table and staring at the microwave oven fearfully.

"This is a *big* problem," Aunt Zelda said after explaining the whole thing to her sister.

Sabrina stood at Aunt Hilda's bedside as Aunt Zelda paced back and forth frantically.

Salem was curled up in a chair in the corner of the room, staring at them with fierce disinterest.

"How *is* Benjie, anyway?" Aunt Hilda asked.

"He's fine, dear," Aunt Zelda said. "But that's the least of our problems now, because—"

Aunt Hilda interrupted, asking, "How's his friend with those awful-smelling whalebone teeth?"

"He's *fine,* Hilda," Aunt Zelda replied. "But we've got a real *problem* to deal with, here, okay?"

Aunt Hilda hiccupped.

Her bedstand disappeared and was replaced by a set of false teeth.

"Oh *no,* Aunt Hilda!" Sabrina exclaimed. "I hope those teeth weren't in someone's *mouth!*"

Aunt Hilda's shoulders hunched as she winced. "I'm sorry!"

"What are we going to *do?*" Sabrina cried. "I mean, we've got Benjamin Franklin in the kitchen . . . and my five library books are stacked up at the Continental Congress in Philadelphia in 1776!"

"Well, for one thing," Aunt Hilda said, "we shouldn't panic."

Aunt Zelda tossed a glaring glance at her and released a single, sharp, *"Hah!"* She continued pacing as she said, "Are you kidding? We've got *plenty* of reasons to panic!"

"Yes," Aunt Hilda said, "but it won't do any good."

"Who *cares?*" Aunt Zelda barked. "First of all, I need to talk with Drell. This is *much* too big for us to handle on our own. I'm sure he'll have some advice."

"Oh, Drell *always* has advice," Aunt Hilda muttered snidely.

Aunt Hilda spun around and faced her. "He's the head of the Witch Council and we need him. Thanks to your hiccups, we have potentially upset American history. We could all disappear at any *second* if history is changed because of the presence of Sabrina's books at the Continental Congress. If one of those men reads one of those books, he might change his *mind!* He might not *sign* the Declaration of Independence! The entire country might disappear in a puff of smoke, all because of the lousy illustrations in those library books!"

Aunt Hilda looked at her sister and said quietly, "Oh . . . well . . . in that case . . . maybe you should talk to Drell."

Aunt Zelda rolled her eyes. "That's what I'm *going* to do. But"—she turned to Sabrina—"in the meantime, you're going to have to keep an eye on Benjie."

Sabrina's mouth dropped open as she gawked at her aunt. "What? *Me?*"

"Yes, you. You're the only other person *here!*" Aunt Zelda exclaimed. "You don't expect me to put Benjie in *Salem's* care, do you?"

"Well, no, but . . . but . . ."

"No buts, Sabrina. I know you have homework to do, but I'm going to *have* to depend on you. This isn't just *any* emergency . . . it's a *family* emergency."

After a moment, Sabrina nodded. "Okay. I'll do whatever I have to do to help."

"Good girl," Aunt Zelda said with a smile. "Thank you."

"But . . . what do you want me to *do* with him?" Sabrina asked.

"Oh, I don't know," Aunt Zelda said, staring at the ceiling thoughtfully as she scratched her head. "He loves to play games. We've got lots of board games in the hall closet. And there's a deck of cards in the drawer of the end table beside the sofa."

"We don't *have* a sofa anymore," Sabrina said.

Aunt Zelda rolled her eyes. "Yes, right, okay . . . there's a deck of cards in the drawer of the end table beside the swing set."

"But . . . what do I *tell* him?" Sabrina asked. "I mean, he keeps asking about how he got here. So, what do I say?"

Aunt Zelda said, "Oh, uh . . . well, uh . . ."

"Tell him he's dreaming," Aunt Hilda said.

Sabrina and Aunt Zelda both flinched as they turned to her.

"I'm not kidding," Aunt Hilda said. "Tell him he's dreaming. Tell him he was, um . . . hit on the head. Yeah. Something fell on his head and he's just dreaming. None of this is real, that's what you should tell him. Then, after Zelda talks to Drell, maybe we can fix it so he never *remembers* any of this."

"Hey, *that's* good," Aunt Zelda said. "You hiccup the entire country into a possible time rip that might wipe out the existence of America as we know it . . . and you have the nerve to put it all on *my* shoulders?"

"Well, it was your idea to talk to Drell!" Aunt Hilda cried.

"But I am *not* the one who guzzled so much Venusian mead that my hiccups became a lethal *weapon!"* Aunt Zelda shouted.

Sabrina leaned her head back and rolled her eyes.

"Hey!" Sabrina barked. "Don't you think we've got enough to worry about right now? I think we should all concentrate on solving our problem . . . we don't have *time* for arguing."

Both of Sabrina's aunts turned to her, startled.

"You're right," Aunt Hilda said. "The sooner this is taken care of, the better. Thank you, Sabrina. Thank goodness at least *one* person in this family is levelheaded," she added with a smug little sniff.

"Personally, I think you're all loopy," Salem muttered. He yawned as he curled up and placed his head on his forepaws. "I've never been so glad I'm just the house cat."

"Okay," Aunt Zelda said, "I'm heading for the linen closet. I'm going to the Other Realm for an emergency meeting with Drell."

Sabrina sighed. "And I suppose that means I have to go downstairs and make sure one of the fathers of our country remains occupied until you get back."

Aunt Zelda smiled. "Yes, something like that. Just don't play Trivial Pursuit, okay? Most of those questions just wouldn't be fair to poor Benjie."

"Well . . . thanks bunches," Sabrina muttered. "I can't wait."

Aunt Zelda left the room with a jovial wave of her hand.

Sabrina turned to Aunt Hilda and said, "I guess I should go downstairs and entertain our guest."

"He's really a very nice guy," Aunt Hilda said. "I'm sure you won't have any problems with him."

Sabrina smiled. "Thanks, Aunt Hilda." She turned and started to leave the bedroom.

"You know, Zelda's probably just jealous," Aunt Hilda said.

Sabrina stopped in the doorway and turned to face her aunt. "What do you mean?"

"I think Zelda was *very* jealous because Benjie was so attracted to me," Aunt Hilda said. "He may not look like much but he's got a *wonderful* mind . . . and he's not a bad kisser, either." Aunt Hilda smiled.

"So I've heard," Sabrina muttered with a smile. She couldn't hold back a giggle as she left the room and headed down the hall. Although they were a bit odd at times, Sabrina took great delight in the fact that her aunts were never boring.

Awaiting her downstairs was one of the most famous fathers of America . . . and it was her job to entertain him.

As she went down the stairs, her stomach shrank, her lungs seemed to close, and her heart thundered against her ribcage. What was she going to say? What was she going to *do?*

Sabrina had no idea.

☆

Chapter 5

☆

"Hello again, Mr. Franklin," Sabrina said, grinning broadly, trying to hide her nervousness.

Franklin smiled at her and immediately stood from his chair. "Hello, young lady," he said with a gentlemanly bow of his head.

"Sabrina," she said. "My name's Sabrina."

"'Tis a pleasure, Sabrina."

She felt her cheeks become hot with a blush. "Thank you, Mr. Franklin," she said through a smile. "So . . . we're gonna have to wait for my aunt Zelda to come back. She's trying to figure out how to, um . . . well, how to send you back to Philadelphia."

"But I still do not understand how I came to be *here*."

Stalling for time, Sabrina pulled out a chair

55

and seated herself at the table. Franklin lowered himself into his chair, waiting for her to respond.

"Well, Mr. Franklin," she said hesitantly, "to tell you the truth . . . I don't really understand it, either. See . . . a *lot* of things happen around here that I don't understand."

"Well, I must confess, I feel much the same way," Franklin said, glancing warily at the microwave oven. "By the way, young lady, what *is* that, that . . . noisy *box?* Earlier, it made a . . . a most *frightful* rumbling."

"Well, that's our micro—" Sabrina stopped herself, realizing that would make no sense to him. Instead, she said, "It's an oven, Mr. Franklin. It heats things up very quickly."

Salem hopped up onto the kitchen table and settled on his haunches, facing Franklin and Sabrina.

"Is that so?" Franklin asked, suddenly staring at the microwave with more interest than fear. He craned his head forward and squinted through his eyeglasses at the oven. "Well, er . . . *how* quickly?"

Sabrina froze in place for a moment, wondering if she was doing the right thing. She was chatting, quite casually, about a microwave oven . . . with a man who had just been unexpectedly jerked from 1776. What if they weren't able to wipe away Franklin's memory before sending him back . . . *if* they were able to send him back. Anything she told him could very possibly have a powerful impact on American history.

At the same time, she realized she could not just tell him to sit there at the table and shut up, not ask any questions. She had to answer at least *some* of his questions . . . didn't she? How could she just stand there with her mouth open, like a fish out of water? Sooner or later, he would realize things weren't as he *knew* them to be . . . so why try to fool him by pretending he was still at home in 1776?

"If you'd like, Mr. Franklin," Sabrina said suddenly, "I'll make you a cup of tea so you can *see* how quickly."

"Oh, yes, uh . . . yes, a cup of tea would be quite nice, thank you," he said, nodding and smiling nervously, glancing a couple times at the microwave.

Sabrina went to the cupboard and got a mug, then went to the sink and filled it with water. When she turned around to take it to the microwave, she was surprised to see Franklin gawking at her in awe, his mouth hanging open.

"Your water," he said breathlessly. "It flows . . . like a stream . . . without being pumped."

She ignored him. She simply wasn't up to getting into the complexities of plumbing. "I'm going to heat up this cup of water in the oven," she said as she popped the microwave open, put the mug inside, and closed the door. It beeped a few times as she touched the appropriate buttons, then began to hum rumblingly when she hit START. She opened a cupboard and scanned the contents as she asked, "What kind of tea would you like, Mr. Franklin? We have Lovely Lemon, Sleepy Cinnamon, Berry Bouquet, and, uh . . . some herbal tea." She turned to him and smiled, waiting for his reply.

His furry white eyebrows curled downward in the middle as his mouth opened and closed a few times. "I-I-I . . . well, I'm not quite sure what—"

"Take the Berry Bouquet," Salem said.

Startled, Franklin jerked around and faced the cat on the table.

"Well, it seems to be the most popular among all our guests," Salem continued earnestly. "And besides . . . everyone *hates* that herbal stuff."

Franklin made a sound that *sounded* like *"Bleck!"* Then he fell over backward in his chair and hit the floor with a loud crack of wood against tile.

"Oh, Mr. Franklin!" Sabrina exclaimed as she rushed to his side.

He rolled off the chair and Sabrina helped him to his feet. "I'm fine, I'm fine," he said. He adjusted his spectacles, then ran a hand back over the balding top of his head. "It's just that . . . I thought I heard . . ." He pointed a quavery finger at Salem.

Salem sat on his haunches and said, "Sorry, I was just trying to be helpful."

"It *spoke!*" he blurted, stumbling backward

from Salem. "The *cat!* It actually *spoke* to me! How could a cat possibly—"

The microwave oven gave a long, shrill beep from behind Franklin, startling him so much that he stumbled forward again toward Salem, who said, "Watch your step!"

Franklin stood in place and stared open-mouthed at Salem, studying the cat. "'Twas real," he whispered, turning to Sabrina. "What kind of witchcraft is it that makes a cat *speak?*"

Sabrina scowled at Salem, muttering, "A lot of help you are."

"You don't find this astonishing, Sabrina?" Franklin asked. His eyes had become bigger around than his spectacles.

"No, not really," she said. Sabrina was a little hesitant to tell Franklin the truth. People from his time period were not known for their civility toward witches. But she figured that anyone who would go out into an electrical storm and fly a kite with a piece of metal attached to it just to see what would happen *had* to have an open mind. She decided to throw caution to the wind and just tell him everything, but not without choosing her words carefully. "If you promise not to burn me at the stake, or anything, I'll tell you the truth, Mr. Franklin. It *is* witchcraft." Her face screwed up slightly as she waited for his response.

Franklin stroked his chin as he stared at the cat thoughtfully. "Hmmm . . . I have never quite believed in all the stories of witches and their spells. But a talking cat . . . that is, indeed, a phenomenon that could be explained by nothing less than witchcraft." He turned to Sabrina again. "You are telling me, young lady, that . . . *you* are a witch?"

She nodded. "So are Aunt Zelda and Aunt Hilda."

"Hilda?"

"Aunt Zelda's sister. She's upstairs in bed. She's, uh . . . not feeling well."

"And does this witchcraft have something to do with my sudden and mysterious disappearance from Philadelphia?"

Sabrina sighed and nodded again. "Why don't you have a seat, Mr. Franklin. I'll fix your tea, and then I'll tell you the whole story."

An hour later, Benjamin Franklin was beating the pants off Sabrina at a game of Monopoly.

"I have enough money to buy . . . Park Place," he said thoughtfully. He cocked a brow at Sabrina. "Is that a good thing to do?"

"Buying Park Place?" Sabrina replied. "Yes, it's a *very* good thing to do." She smiled and shook her head. Franklin already had Boardwalk, Marvin Gardens, four hotels, and all the railroads.

Over tea at the kitchen table, Sabrina had told Franklin all about Aunt Hilda's magical hiccups, that they had transported him from 1776 to 1997. She hadn't told him about her library books having been transported from 1997 to

1776; as long as he'd understood what had happened to him, she'd seen no sense in going into annoying, tedious, and possibly history-shattering details.

Franklin had not doubted her for a moment. He had been very interested in everything she had to say. When she had finished, he'd remained silent for a long time, then asked, "If this is 1997, and I am in America . . . then America has been in existence for two hundred and twenty-one years. Please tell me, Sabrina . . . how is it?"

"I beg your pardon?" she'd asked.

"This country . . . what is it like? Did we make the right decisions in constructing our document? Did we err in any way?"

"Well . . . people complain about taxes a lot and Beavis and Butthead got their own movie . . . but people in every other country in the world want to come here. There are fourteen hundred channels available on satellite, and you can usually find a grocery store open at any hour, so . . . overall, I'd say you did a pretty good job."

But he'd not been satisfied with that. Franklin had wanted to know specifics. What was the tone of the country, what kind of personality did it have, what was important to its citizens?

At first, Sabrina hadn't been sure how to answer those questions. Then she remembered that Aunt Zelda had told her "Benjie" liked to play games.

"You *really* want to know what's important in America?" she'd asked. "Let's play Monopoly."

She'd brought out the board, put it on the kitchen table, and explained the object and rules to Franklin. He'd picked up on the game immediately and had expressed great delight in each of his victories . . . and there had been *plenty* of those.

For the time being, Sabrina was stuck in jail.

As they continued playing, Sabrina said, "Could I ask you a favor, Mr. Franklin?"

"A favor? If it is within my power, I would be honored."

"I'm supposed to write a paper about you for one of my classes in school."

"A paper? About me?" He squinted curiously at her through his spectacles.

"Yes, for American History class. We're supposed to write about one of the men who signed the Declaration of Independence, and I chose you."

Franklin suddenly lost interest in the game and leaned back in his chair. "You mean to say . . . students speak of me in school? They read of me?"

"And write of you . . . which is what I'm gonna be doing. I was just wondering if you'd be willing . . . well, I mean, as long as you're here . . . would you mind answering some questions for me? You could *really* help me make that paper accurate. In fact, I think it's safe to say I'd have the most accurate paper in class."

A smile grew slowly on his broad face, and he pulled in his chin, making the pocket of flesh beneath it swell roundly. Placing a hand to his chest, he said, "I am *flattered* you chose to write of me, Sabrina. And I would be honored to help you in any way I can. Tell me . . . what details do you plan to include in this document?"

"Oh, you know . . . stuff about your child-hood, how you became—"

The doorbell rang.

Sabrina froze in mid-sentence.

"What was that lovely sound?" Franklin asked.

"Uuuhhh . . ."

It rang again.

Who would be at the door tonight? Sabrina wondered. Her mind raced as she went over possible visitors. It was nobody in the family . . . they usually just *popped* in. That meant it was someone who would most likely not understand the presence of Benjamin Franklin in the kitchen.

As the bell rang again, Sabrina wondered, *Okay, so* now *what do I do?*

Chapter 6

'Tis a *lovely* sound," Franklin said when he heard the doorbell again. "Is it a clock?"

"No, that's the doorbell," Sabrina said, standing. "It means there's someone at the door."

"Well, I am certainly interested in meeting some more American citizens from 1997," Franklin said with an eager smile.

"Yes, but Mr. Franklin, I'm not sure how they'd handle meeting *you*. Look . . . the people who know my aunts and me . . . they don't *know* we're witches," she said, speaking her last five words in a whisper.

Franklin tilted his head back as realization dawned in his eyes. "Ah, I see. They would not, then, understand the presence of someone from 1776 in your home. Correct?"

"Very correct, yes."

Franklin scooted his chair back and stood. "I would be happy to make myself scarce, if that would help."

"Oh, thank you, Mr. Franklin. If you'd just stay right here and not move, that would help a lot."

"Gladly," he said, returning to his chair. He leaned down and looked under the table. "Perhaps I could have a conversation with the cat . . . if I can find him. Where did he go?"

The doorbell rang again.

"Salem!" Sabrina called.

The cat sauntered into the kitchen and hopped up on the table, saying to Sabrina, "I hope you haven't called me back here just to scold me some more."

"No, Salem, just keep Mr. Franklin company, okay? I've got to answer the door."

"No problem at all," Salem said, curling up on the table in front of Franklin. "So . . . seen any good movies lately?"

Sabrina hurried out of the kitchen and went to the front door. She opened it to see Jenny standing on the porch.

"Hey, what's up?" Sabrina asked.

Jenny stood motionless on the porch, staring openmouthed at Sabrina. She blinked a few times, then said, "Uuuhhh . . . Sabrina?"

"Yeah."

"Can I, uh . . . ask you a question?"

"Sure."

"Why am I standing on your porch?"

Alarms went off in Sabrina's head. Jenny looked dazed and confused, and if she didn't know why she was standing on Sabrina's porch, then something was very wrong.

"Hey, are you all right?" Sabrina asked. "C'mon inside."

Jenny walked slowly through the door and Sabrina closed it.

"I don't *know* why you're here," Sabrina said, turning to Jenny. "Where did you come from?"

"Come from?" Jenny asked. "Well . . . the Slicery."

"Why?" Sabrina asked.

"Why what?"

"Why did you come over here from the Slicery?"

"Well . . . I *didn't*. One minute, I was in the Slicery playing Foosball, and then . . . I was standing on your porch."

Sabrina began to get *very* worried. This was beginning to sound like all the other weird things that had been happening all day. But why would one of Aunt Hilda's hiccups simply transport Jenny from the Slicery to the front porch? So far, Aunt Hilda's hiccups had been making things trade places . . . they hadn't moved things or people from one place or another without some kind of trade.

"Are you sure you didn't *walk* over here?" Sabrina asked.

"Walk?" Jenny looked around as if she were in

a foreign country. "No, I didn't walk. I was . . . I was playing *Foosball!*"

"Okay, Jenny, why don't you come in and sit down and I'll get you a—"

"What did you call me?" Jenny asked. Her face had suddenly come alive with shock and disbelief.

"Uh . . . I called you, um . . . *Jenny.* That *is* your name, right?"

Jenny flinched and took a step backward away from Sabrina. "Is that some kinda *joke?"*

"What?" Sabrina asked. She suddenly felt more confused than Jenny had looked.

"Look, Sabrina, I'm confused enough. Don't make it worse by calling me 'Jenny.' I mean, I know you're just trying to be funny, but I'm not laughing, okay?"

"Well . . . what would you *like* me to call you?"

Jenny rolled her eyes and said, "I'd like you to call me by my *name,* okay? *Harvey."*

"Uh . . . Huh-H-Harvey?"

"Well, *yeah!"* Jenny looked annoyed for a moment. But that look of annoyance soon became one of fear. "Why're you lookin' at me like that, Sabrina?"

"I don't, uh . . . I don't know. Exactly. Uh . . . you're *Harvey?"* Sabrina was beginning to feel dizzy with confusion.

"Yes, I'm Harvey!"

"Then I'm guessing you haven't, um . . . looked in a mirror lately."

"What do you mean?" Jenny asked, looking very worried.

"Harvey, have you, um . . . you *are* Harvey, right?" Sabrina asked, just to make sure.

"Sabrina, what's *wrong* with you? Of *course* I'm Harvey!"

Sabrina froze, wide-eyed and afraid of whatever it was this whole conversation was leading up to. "Haven't you listened to your own *voice?*"

"What do you *mean,* haven't I listened to my own—" Jenny interrupted herself with a gasp and slapped a hand over her mouth.

Sabrina and Jenny stared at one another for a long silent moment. All the while, Sabrina wondered if Jenny was going through some kind of breakdown . . . or if that really *was* Harvey inside Jenny's body.

"That's *Jenny's* voice!" Jenny hissed. "Sabrina . . . what's *happened* to me?"

Sabrina was still confused and didn't know how to react. Just to make sure, she asked a revealing question:

"Do you think Libby's a nice girl who's just misunderstood by some people?"

Jenny frowned. "Of course she's a nice girl. Jenny's just upset with Libby because she spilled that grape juice on her."

"Oh, boy," Sabrina muttered to herself. "You *are* Harvey!" Sabrina knew that in her current mood, Jenny would *never* say that Libby was a nice girl, not to *anyone,* not even as a *joke.* "Harvey, what's *happened* to you?"

Harvey lowered his head very, very slowly and looked down at his body . . . which was actually *Jenny's* body, dressed in jeans, a green T-shirt, and a denim vest.

"Aaack!" he blurted, throwing himself backward against the front door. "I'm a *girl!*" he screamed. In his panic, he began to breathe heavily and his eyes resembled those of a horse surrounded by rattlesnakes.

"Calm down, Harvey, okay? Just calm *down!*" Sabrina hurried to him, put her hands on his shoulders and began patting them comfortingly.

Sabrina's mind raced to find some reason for this bizarre development in her life, which was already bizarre enough as far as she was concerned. She really *did* believe she was dealing with Harvey and not Jenny. But if one of Aunt Hilda's hiccups were responsible for this, then that could only mean that Jenny was inside Harvey's body! Sabrina tried to figure out why Aunt Hilda would *ever* think of Jenny and Harvey—as she had thought of Sabrina's lunch or the cow she'd dreamed of—and came up with nothing. And then . . .

. . . she remembered telling Aunt Hilda about the fight Jenny and Harvey were having. Sabrina had explained the whole situation to Aunt Hilda . . . and apparently, the whole situation had flitted through Aunt Hilda's mind again . . . at about the time another hiccup came along, no doubt.

That meant Jenny was standing in the Slicery,

probably at the Foosball table, feeling very, *very* confused inside Harvey's body. She was probably going absolutely *nuts* by now!

Sabrina took Jenny's hand . . . which, for the time being, was really *Harvey's* hand . . . and said, "C'mon, *Harvey,* let's go into the living room."

"Sabrina," Harvey whined in Jenny's voice, "what's *happened* to me? What's going *on?*"

Sabrina led Harvey into the living room and over to the swing set.

"Sit here, Harvey."

"But, Sabrina, I've got Jenny's *body!* Hey . . . is this a *swing* in your *living* room? *Cool!*"

"Yep, it's a swing, so just sit in it, okay?" She pushed him down into one of the swing seats, then got behind him and pushed. "You just swing for a while. Just relax and swing." She pushed him again.

The chains made a high-pitched squeak as Harvey swung back and forth in Jenny's body.

"You just keep relaxing and swinging, Harvey," Sabrina said, walking around in front of Harvey. "I'll be right back, okay? You understand me? I'll be *right back.* Do *not* leave that swing!"

Sabrina hurried out of the living room and into the kitchen, where Salem was sitting on the kitchen table facing Franklin.

"You have *got* to be *kidding!*" Salem was saying. "You actually prefer vanilla to chocolate?"

"But the vanilla has such a delightfully *subtle* flavor," Franklin replied. "It's flavor is *suggested* rather than asserted. Chocolate, on the other hand, is overwhelming, and rather—"

"Be right back, nobody move!" Sabrina called as she raced out of the kitchen and upstairs to Aunt Hilda's room.

When Sabrina walked into the bedroom, Aunt Hilda was lying still on the bed, eyes closed, snoring quietly. She remembered the theory that a good scare could bring hiccups to a halt, and decided to try it again.

Sabrina went to Aunt Hilda's bedside, reached down and shook her once, then stepped back and waved her hand as Aunt Hilda awoke with a start and turned toward her.

By the time Aunt Hilda awoke, Sabrina had turned herself into Richard Simmons, wearing a pair of short shorts and a tank top sparkling with sequins.

"Move that booty!" Richard Simmons cried. "Come on! Outta bed! Let's do it! Let's *stretch* and *bend* and *stretch* and *bend* and *stretch* and *bend* and—"

Aunt Hilda hid her face with her hands and released a shrill scream.

"C'mon, outta that bed!" Richard Simmons shouted. "Let's sweat to the oldies!"

Aunt Hilda continued to scream and scream . . . until she hiccuped.

Sabrina waved an arm and became herself again, then sat on the edge of her aunt's bed.

"Sorry, Aunt Hilda," she said. "I just thought I'd try to scare you again."

"Well, it *did* work," Hilda said, slumping against her pillows and sighing with relief. "You scared the *sweat* out of me! But obviously"—she hiccupped again—"it didn't stop the hiccups."

"Aunt Hilda, our problems have gotten bigger all of a sudden."

"What? What do you mean?"

Sabrina explained to her that Harvey and Jenny had apparently exchanged bodies due to one of her hiccups.

"Oh, dear," Aunt Hilda whispered. "Did *I* do that?"

"Yes. And I'm sure you didn't even realize you were doing it. I told you about the argument they had, and you probably thought about it for just a second . . . right about the time you hiccupped."

"I'm *so* sorry, Sabrina!"

"Look, don't worry about it!" Sabrina said. "I know you didn't do it intentionally. But now . . . I'm wondering what *I* should do!"

Aunt Hilda thought for a moment, then said, "I could try to reverse it!"

"What? *How?*"

"I could think about Harvey and Jenny until I hiccup again!" She held up a hand and said, "Hush, dear." She closed her eyes and remained still for a long moment, until . . . she hiccupped so hard that the bedsprings squealed and the frame creaked. Her eyes snapped open and she grinned, saying, *"There!* I was thinking about

Harvey and Jenny when I hiccupped that time, so they *must* have switched back!"

Jenny appeared in the bedroom's open door and said, "Sabrina . . . I can't take this. I gotta get back into my own body. I mean . . . this is makin' me *nuts!*"

Aunt Hilda's face drooped into an expression of defeat.

Sabrina looked down at her and asked, "Aunt Hilda, what am I gonna *do?*"

"Well," Hilda said, "the *first* thing you've got to do is go out and find Harvey's body! Bring them both back here and don't let them out of your sight until Zelda gets back with somebody who can *cure* this thing!"

"But I'm already watching over Mr. Franklin!" Sabrina exclaimed. "I can only do so much!"

"Well . . ." Hilda thought a moment. "You could always put him into some decent clothes and take him with you. But I bet if you put him in front of the television, you could leave without worrying about him going anywhere. He's really big on new stuff. He's more curious than a *cat!*"

"Okay, whatever," Sabrina said, walking toward Harvey. "I'll do one or the other. You just stay in bed and wait for Aunt Zelda to come back."

Hilda said, "That's what I was *doing,* until you woke me up with your little Richard Simmons trick!"

Sabrina ignored her, took Harvey's arm, and led him down the hall, saying, "C'mon, Harvey, let's go downstairs. Don't worry, we're gonna work this out."

They went downstairs and into the kitchen. But the kitchen was empty. Franklin and Salem were gone.

Sabrina stared at the abandoned table with a feeling of panic swelling in her chest . . . until she heard raucous laughter coming from the living room. Still clutching the elbow of Jenny's body, which contained Harvey, she left the kitchen and went into the living room.

Franklin sat in the recliner, laughing hysterically at the television, stomping his foot and slapping his knee. Salem lay on the floor in front of him, curled around the television's remote control. Sabrina looked at the television and saw the logo in the lower right corner of the screen . . . Franklin was watching and laughing at C-SPAN.

"Okay," Sabrina said, "what's going on?"

Salem bounced to his feet and spun around to face her, saying, "Hey, I'm only a cat! There's a limit to my conversational abilities with one of the fathers of our country, so . . . I thought he might like to watch some TV!"

"Can you keep an eye on him for me, Salem?" Sabrina asked. "I've gotta leave for a little bit."

"Sure. He seems to be enjoying himself."

Franklin burst into another round of rowdy

laughter. "Oh, this is *rich!*" he cried, grinning at Sabrina. "This is really quite comical!"

"Did the cat just talk?" Jenny's question reminded Sabrina of the urgency of the situation.

Heading for the door, she said, "C'mon, Jenny, we've—"

"You mean *Harvey,*" Jenny said.

"Harvey, yes, Harvey. We've gotta get over to the Slicery and find Harvey."

"You mean *Jenny,*" Jenny said.

"Yes, Jenny, Jenny. *Sheesh!*" She looked over her shoulder and said, "I'm taking Aunt Zelda's car, in case she asks." Then she led Jenny/ Harvey out of the house, just as Jenny/Harvey started to ask, "Hey, who's the guy wearing the funny—"

Salem hunkered down beside the remote control.

"Hey, check this out, Benjie," he said, poking two of the buttons with his paw. C-SPAN was replaced by the History Channel. "You guys have got your own cable channel now!"

☆

Chapter 7

☆

Salem and Franklin lounged in front of the television. Franklin was in the recliner, and Salem was on the floor with the remote, surfing channels. He stopped now and then, when he thought he'd found something that might interest Franklin. At the moment, Salem was trying to explain *Wheel of Fortune* to the man whose face adorns the one hundred–dollar bill.

"I am not certain I understand," Franklin said, scratching his head. "You win money by correctly choosing a consonant used in the puzzle . . . but you must *pay* to receive a vowel?"

"Yep," Salem said.

"But what if the vowel you request is not there?"

"You still lose your money."

Franklin tilted his head curiously. "And where does all that money go?"

"Well, I can't *prove* it," Salem said, lowering his voice to a conspiratorial whisper, "but I have it on good authority that all the money spent on vowels goes straight into Vanna's wardrobe. At least, that's what I heard on E!"

Salem poked at the remote and began flipping from channel to channel. He stopped on a black-and-white image of a young Ronald Reagan sharing the screen with a chimpanzee.

"Bedtime for Bonzo!" Salem exclaimed. "Look, Benjie! There's our fortieth president!"

"President?" Franklin muttered, frowning at the television. "President of what?"

"The United States. Ronald Reagan. He started out as an actor, but when he couldn't get any more acting jobs, he went into politics. As an actor, he couldn't get arrested, but as a politician . . . well, he kinda won the Oscar, if you know what I mean."

Franklin was still frowning, leaning forward in his chair. "And . . . the monkey?"

"I don't know *what* the monkey's doing these days. Probably living with Michael Jackson."

The doorbell rang and Franklin smiled. "Such a pleasant sound," he said.

"Uh-oh," Salem said. "Depending on who that is, we could have a problem."

The doorbell rang again.

"Oh, dear," Franklin said, turning to Salem. "We're the only ones here, aren't we?"

"I'm afraid so," Salem whispered. "Maybe you should hold it down until—"

Franklin stood and started across the living room, toward the door.

"No!" Salem cried, running after him. "That's not a good idea, Benjie. I don't think you should—"

"Nonsense," Franklin said. "I am perfectly capable of answering a door. They can't have changed *that* much. No sense in making a visitor stand out on the porch all night."

As Franklin opened the door, Salem skidded to a slippery halt on the tile floor. The cat looked up and saw Mr. Snodgrass, the next door neighbor, standing on the porch.

Phil Snodgrass was in his mid-fifties and balding, with a big belly. He wore a pair of enormously baggy blue shorts that billowed around his knobby, sticklike legs. There was a round-headed bug-eyed alien on his white T-shirt, and beneath the alien's face was written: WE ARE NOT ALONE. He wore a green fishing cap with several lures and homemade flies stuck in the sides. He held a can of generic soda in one hand—the can was white with COLA written in black letters—and a stubby, stinky cigar between the first two knuckles of his other hand.

"Uh, hiya, there," Mr. Snodgrass said, nodding.

"Hello," Franklin said, smiling.

Salem looked up to see that Franklin was staring at Mr. Snodgrass with an expression of utter fascination, the way someone might stare at the first alien to step out of the mother ship. But Franklin was not staring at a space alien . . . he was staring at a citizen of 1997, of a country Franklin had helped to create. Salem thought it was unfortunate that the first person Franklin was meeting outside of the Spellman house was Mr. Snodgrass, who was a bit of a moron.

"I was wonderin', uh, if one of the ladies was home, 'cause, uh . . .." He reached around and scratched the back of his neck, lifting the bottom of his T-shirt up over the bottom half of his large belly. ". . . Well, seems you got a cow in your backyard. And I think there's one in the yard on the other side of your house. Did you know that?"

"A cow?" Franklin said.

"Yep. It's mooin' up a storm behind your house. You didn't know?"

"I was not aware of it, no," Franklin replied.

Salem paced frantically around Franklin's heels, his eyes wide with panic. He was about to start biting Franklin's ankles, when the cat was struck with an idea. He turned and ran down the hall, skidding to a stop around the corner. He peered back down the hall and called, in his best feminine voice, "Is that you, Mr. Snodgrass? Don't you worry about those cows, now. We're babysitting them for the night along with our neighbor. They'll be gone tomorrow!"

Mr. Snodgrass leaned forward and poked his head in the door. "Uh . . . okay, if you say so. But they're awful *noisy* cows, you know what I mean?"

Salem shouted down the hall, "I'll go outside and do my best to quiet her down, Mr. Snodgrass. The other one, too. They like music. Brahms, mostly! I'll get the boombox and see if I can calm them down."

Nodding, Mr. Snodgrass pulled his head out of the doorway and looked at Franklin again. "You a relative?"

"No, a visitor," Franklin replied. "From Philadelphia."

Salem trotted down the hall and started biting at Franklin's ankles.

"Oh, nice to meetcha," Mr. Snodgrass said. He grabbed Franklin's hand and shook it firmly. "Phil Snodgrass. I live next door. I got a welding shop in town."

"Ah, how nice." Franklin looked down at Salem and muttered, "Stop that," as he pushed the cat away with a foot. He returned his attention to Mr. Snodgrass.

Salem's nerves were buzzing. He knew that Benjie would start talking craziness any minute—at least, it would *sound* like craziness to Mr. Snodgrass—and Salem *had* to get him back inside and get that door shut and locked. He couldn't *talk* in front of Mr. Snodgrass, so Salem did the next best thing. He started to meow. It wasn't just *any* meow, though . . . it was a high, yowling cry of desperation.

"Gotta real upset cat, there," said Mr. Snodgrass.

"Yes, I'm afraid so," Franklin said.

"It was my cat, I'd kick its tail up around its whiskers, caterwaulin' like that."

Salem fell silent for a moment, turned to Mr. Snodgrass, and hissed unpleasantly. Then he continued meowing.

Mr. Snodgrass took a swig of his soda, then asked, "What'd you say your name was?"

"I'm afraid I didn't. I am Benja—*ack!*" Franklin yelped, because Salem had begun to use his leg for a scratching post. Franklin bent down and tried to push Salem away.

"You should have that cat fixed, Benjie," Mr. Snodgrass said, flinching as Salem spit at him viciously.

Franklin picked Salem up in his arms, saying, "I think he just wants some attention."

"What I want," Salem whispered into Franklin's ear, "is for you to come inside and close the door. *Now!*"

"So, you gonna do any fishing while you're here, Benjie?" Mr. Snodgrass asked.

"Well, er, this was a bit of a surprise trip, I'm

afraid," Franklin sputtered. "I haven't done much in the way of planning."

"You havin' a costume party in there?" Mr. Snodgrass asked, poking his cigar over Franklin's shoulder.

"No. Why, Mr. Snodgrass? Were you looking for one?"

"Oh, no, it's just that . . . well, you're dressed kinda funny."

Franklin blinked with surprise. "I am?" he asked, looking at the alien face on Mr. Snodgrass's T-shirt.

"Oh, well," Mr. Snodgrass said with a smile and a shrug. "To each his own. Hey, tell you what. I got the garage open next door. I'm tyin' some flies. My oldest son and I are goin' fishin' in the mornin'. You wanna come over and join me, you're welcome," he said. He turned and started to walk away. "If not, nice to meetcha!"

"Now let's get inside!" Salem whispered. "Before he thinks of something else to say!"

Franklin stepped back and closed the door. "Tell me, Salem," he said as he placed the cat on the floor. "Would you consider Mr. Snodgrass to be . . . shall we say *typical*? Yes, do you think he is a *typical* American?"

Salem sauntered back into the living room, saying, "I hate to be the one to tell you this, Benjie, but . . . yes. I'm afraid so."

"So, it would be safe to say, then," Franklin continued, "that Mr. Snodgrass's opinions on the topics of the day would be those of an average American?"

"Frightening, isn't it?" Salem curled up around the remote control again, much more relaxed now that Benjie was inside, the door was closed, and the danger had passed. "You should listen to talk radio," the cat continued. "It's like the Phil Snodgrass Show, twenty-four hours a day, on almost every station." Salem punched the remote again and again, surfing through the channels, until he finally stopped on The Learning Channel. They were showing a documentary on cat shows. Salem's attention was riveted on a sultry Persian with a sparkling collar. "Oh, baby," Salem muttered. "This is better than *Baywatch!*"

When the show finally broke for a commercial, Salem looked up at the chair and was about to speak . . . but Franklin wasn't there.

"Benjie?" Salem said. He stood, turned, and raised his voice as he looked around the room: *"Benjie? Where'd you go?"* Salem did not see him in the living room, so he headed for the kitchen.

"Did you get hungry?" Salem shouted, so Franklin would hear him in the kitchen. "We don't have much food in the house, you know, because the refrigerator turned into a cow this morning. Overall, it hasn't been such a good day for *anybody* in this house, so if I were you, I wouldn't feel so bad about being catapulted into the—" Salem froze in the kitchen. It was empty. "—future," he whimpered. *"Benjiiieee!"* Salem cried as he ran through the entire house as only a cat can.

He darted over furniture, up curtains, under furniture, down curtains, surfing rugs over hardwood floors, and occasionally defying two or three of the laws of physics, until he'd been through every room in the house.

Franklin wasn't in any of them. But Hilda was in her bedroom.

"What is the *matter* with you, Salem?" Hilda asked, sitting up in her bed.

Salem did not reply as he looked around the room, checked the closet, looked under the bed.

"Is something wrong, Salem? Has something *happened?"*

"Yes."

"What is it? Did I hiccup something again?"

"I don't have time," Salem said on his way out.

Hilda waved her hand and Salem was suddenly surrounded by sparkling flashes of multicolored light as he froze in place. He levitated off the floor and floated over to Hilda's lap, where the glimmering light disappeared.

"You keep forgetting you're just a *cat,* Salem. Now, I want you to tell me what's going on and"— the bed jolted beneath an epic hiccup— "I want you to tell me the truth!"

"The truth?" Salem said in his best Jack Nicholson voice. "You can't *handle* the truth!" Then he hopped off the bed, landed halfway across the room, and shot out the door.

Hilda made a whimpering sound, then hiccupped again.

Chapter 8

Sabrina drove Harvey (in Jenny's body) to the Slicery in Aunt Zelda's car. In the restaurant, Sabrina spotted Jenny (in Harvey's body) way in the back by the video games, huddling in a corner, back pressed against the wall. He looked terrified. Sabrina and Jenny hurried across the restaurant to him.

"Harvey!" Sabrina exclaimed.

"What?" Jenny replied.

"No, not you," Sabrina said. *"That* Harvey." Sabrina hunkered down in front of him and took his hand.

Harvey's eyes were huge and his lips were trembling.

"Jenny?" Sabrina asked quietly.

"Sabrina?" Harvey whispered. "What's *happened* to me?"

"It's a long story, Jenny. Don't worry, your real body's fine. Harvey's in it."

"Oh, *no!*"

"C'mon, Jenny, we need to go back to my house, okay?"

"I don't know if I can walk in this thing," Jenny said, struggling to stand up in Harvey's body. "It's so *heavy!*"

As Sabrina left the Slicery with Jenny/Harvey and Harvey/Jenny, Benjamin Franklin sat on a barrel in Phil Snodgrass's cluttered but well-lighted garage. There was a refrigerator against the back wall and from it, Mr. Snodgrass removed two cans of generic cola. He handed one can to Franklin, who took a while to figure out how to open it. Mr. Snodgrass didn't notice; he'd returned his attention to the contents of his tackle box, which were spread over an old netless Ping-Pong table.

As Mr. Snodgrass made lures and tied flies, they talked. More accurately, Franklin posed a question occasionally, then listened to Mr. Snodgrass talk.

"I tie all my own flies, make all my own lures," Mr. Snodgrass said. "Always have. Taught both my sons to fish. My oldest boy's the only one who took to it, though. His name's Steve. He's coming over first thing in the morning and we're gonna go out on the lake."

"What about your other boy?" Franklin asked.

"You mean Chuck? Oh, he's a bum. Long hair, beard. Looks like he should be in one of them MTV rock bands, or something. I dunno . . . they both grew up in the same house. My oldest boy's a fisherman and a hunter . . . and my younger one hangs out with weird people who drive motorcycles."

The conversation moved to sports, all of which was gibberish to Franklin. But he brightened when the topics of taxes and politics came up. He took advantage of the subject and said, "Tell me, Mr. Snodgrass, exactly how do you feel about this country? On the whole, I mean."

"This country? It's the best country in the whole world and I'm grateful to be livin' here." He finished up a lure, then dropped it into the tackle box, turning to Franklin again. "Now, if we could just get rid of the government, it'd be perfect!"

"What?" Franklin blurted, startled. "Get rid of the *government?*"

"Yep. Well, you know how it is, Benjie. They've gotten too big for their britches."

"But, that would be . . . *anarchy.*"

"Oh, no, nothin' like that. Who wants a king and queen sittin' on a throne?"

Confused, Franklin frowned and scratched his head. "Do you mean . . . a *monarchy?*"

"Well, that's what we're *talkin'* about, ain't it?" He started working on another lure. "No, we could keep the same basic system. We just start all over again with new blood. We need to put real patriots in office, men with pride in their country, men who understand the values of the common American. What we *really* need in the White House is another man like Ronald Reagan."

Franklin's eyebrows popped up above his spectacles. "The man with the monkey?"

Mr. Snodgrass squinted at Franklin across the Ping-Pong table. "Huh?"

"Ronald Reagan. He *is* the man with the monkey, correct?"

Mr. Snodgrass frowned disapprovingly. "You get hit in the head real hard recently, Benjie?"

A noise like thunder began to grow louder and louder outside the garage, until four large, roaring motorcycles pulled into the driveway.

The noise was so loud that it terrified Franklin. He feared the garage would collapse around him with all that horrible rumbling and growling. When he saw the motorcycles, he stared at them in wonder.

"Oh, brother," Mr. Snodgrass grumbled. "That's my bum son. The one who hates fishing."

"What is he *riding?*" Franklin asked in a hoarse, stunned voice. He slid off the barrel and stood up straight.

"His hog," Mr. Snodgrass said bitterly but casually, without looking at Franklin.

"That's a *hog?*" Franklin asked, placing his hands over his cheeks.

Mr. Snodgrass ignored him and headed out of the garage to meet his son and his son's friends.

"My *goodness!*" Franklin said in little more than a whisper. "What on *earth* have you people done to the *pigs?*"

Franklin followed Mr. Snodgrass out of the garage, stopping just outside the large open door. Once the motorcycles' engines were killed, Franklin felt a bit more comfortable . . . but the two-wheeled machines left such a noxious stench in the air! As Mr. Snodgrass began to talk to the young men on the "hogs," Franklin walked toward them slowly, cautiously.

All four had long, bushy hair. They wore black leather jackets over what appeared to be tight white nightshirts, and black jeans with black leather boots.

"Benjie, this is my son Todd," Mr. Snodgrass said uncomfortably.

"My name's not Todd," he said abruptly in a high-pitched voice. As he bowed his head in greeting, his voice became low and breathy. "It's Wolverine."

Mr. Snodgrass rolled his eyes and said, "Oh, for crying out loud, Todd, don't start *that*. Benjie here's visiting from Philadelphia; you want him to think we're all a bunch of wackos around here?"

Wolverine stepped over to Franklin and they shook hands. Franklin got a good look at the young man's face and saw that his left eyebrow was pierced three times, his nose twice, and his lower lip once.

"What the devil happened to your face?" Franklin asked with a gasp.

"I choose to wear my inner scars and wounds on the outside so people will know me by them," Wolverine said.

Mr. Snodgrass shook his head as he chuckled and said, "He chooses to follow all his nutburger friends like a lemming!"

Franklin ignored him and asked Wolverine, "So, you voluntarily gouged those bits of metal into your face as . . . as a form of expression?"

"Yes. It's a free country, isn't it?"

After a long moment, Franklin laughed and nodded, grinning as he said, "Yes, yes, I suppose it is!"

On the way home, Sabrina told Harvey and Jenny they were dreaming. It was the only thing she could come up with, but she figured it would work . . . at least until Dr. Firehosen, or whatever his name was, was found and could erase their memories of the whole experience.

"We're dreaming?" Harvey asked with Jenny's voice. *"Both* of us? You mean, we're both having the *same* dream?"

"Well, *one* of you is dreaming," Sabrina said with a shrug. "I know it's not me."

"Okay, pinch me," Jenny said, lifting Harvey's arm.

"Pinch you?" Harvey asked.

"Yes! If this is a dream, I want it to end *now!* I'm sick of your unbrushed teeth in my mouth! They feel *carpeted."*

Using Jenny's hand, Harvey pinched the arm in front of him . . . his *own.*

"Ouch!" Jenny cried.

"That's what you get for insulting my teeth," Harvey said. "I brush them *regularly!"*

"What, *weekly?"* Jenny said with a sour look on Harvey's face.

"C'mon, you guys, *stop* it, okay?" Sabrina said. "Now, listen to me very carefully, both of you. I know this is *really* weird and creepy for you both, and you're having a hard time adjusting, but you *can't* let *anyone* know that something's wrong, okay? For now . . . I mean, for as long as you're having this dream . . . you've gotta pretend to be each other. So, no matter what, do *not* answer to your own name, okay?"

They muttered their agreement.

"Thank you. Just . . . try not to say anything to anybody unless you absolutely have to."

About a half mile from home, four motorcycles roared by in the opposite lane, driven by long-haired guys in black leather and jeans and T-shirts. On the lead motorcycle, a passenger clung to the driver's waist for dear life. The passenger was dressed differently from the others, and although he was balding on top, his long light-colored hair flew in the breeze. Someone in the group was laughing hysterically, but the sound was gone in an instant as the motorcycles shot by.

But something about that passenger on the lead motorcycle made Sabrina frown. It looked familiar. In fact, it *almost* looked like . . .

"No, no," she muttered to herself. "It couldn't have been. Salem wouldn't let that happen."

"What?" Jenny and Harvey said simultaneously.

"Oh . . . nothing," Sabrina replied, shaking her head. "I was just hoping our cat hasn't let the Benjie outta the bag."

When Sabrina walked in the front door with Jenny and Harvey, Salem shot toward them like a bullet. Sabrina knew instantly that something was wrong . . . because Salem *never* greeted *anyone* with that much enthusiasm.

Salem pressed a paw to Sabrina's shin twice, then turned and hurried into the kitchen.

"Be right back, you guys," Sabrina said. "Just stay right there."

By the time Sabrina got into the kitchen, Salem had hopped up onto the island in the center of the room. He started babbling incoherently. "We gotta get outside because somebody knocked on the door and Ronald Reagan didn't interest him so he got up and answered and—"

Sabrina held up a hand and said, "Whoa, Salem! Slow down so I can figure out what you're talking about."

In the living room, Jenny and Harvey heard two voices coming from the kitchen.

"Who's she talking to?" Jenny asked with Harvey's voice.

"I don't know," Harvey said, shrugging Jenny's shoulders. "Maybe she's talking to the cat."

"What?" Jenny asked, fidgeting uncomfortably in Harvey's body. "Don't talk craziness."

"Well, it *is* a dream, right?" Harvey asked. "And I *think* I heard the cat talking earlier."

"You're nuts."

"No . . . I'm hungry."

"Well don't *eat* anything!" Jenny said with Harvey's voice. "Remember, that's *my* body, and I don't want you putting *any* weight on it!"

In the kitchen, Sabrina got Salem to explain things to her clearly. The more Salem talked, the more horrified Sabrina looked, until she finally interrupted him and blurted, "Where'd he go, Salem, where'd he *go?*"

"I don't know! He closed the door, so I couldn't follow him! I've been trying to find a way out of here ever since!"

"We've gotta go look for him!" Sabrina said. "Come with me, and keep quiet." Sabrina went into the living room with Salem right behind her. "You two stay right here, understand? Don't answer the phone or the door, and don't *go* anywhere! I'll be back."

Sabrina hurried out of the house with Salem on her heels.

"She's going somewhere with the cat?" Harvey asked with Jenny's voice. "Where would she be going with the cat?"

"I don't know," Jenny said, shrugging Harvey's shoulders. "It doesn't make sense. But, then . . . it's a dream, right?"

Chapter 9

☆

It's so dark in here," Franklin said as he followed Wolverine and the others into a techno club exclusively for teenagers called TeenTech. The thunderous beat of the music was disturbing to Franklin, and he flinched with each floor-shaking thump. He looked at the young people on the dance floor. He watched them jumping and shaking to that pounding beat, and frowned. He turned to Wolverine and shouted to be heard above all the noise.

"Are those young people all right?" Franklin asked.

"Sure," Wolverine said. "They're just dancing."

"Oh!" Franklin said, turning to the dance

floor again. "My, my, my. Dancing has certainly . . . *changed.*"

Franklin sat at a table with Wolverine and his
friends. Franklin watched with fascination as
red and purple laser lights cut through the darkness high above them. He wondered if he'd
made a mistake in coming. But he'd found
Wolverine so *fascinating* . . . not to mention
those two-wheel carriages with no horses! He
couldn't *resist* taking a ride on one of them!

Earlier, Wolverine had introduced Franklin to
his three friends as they stood in front of Mr.
Snodgrass's house. "Benjie, this is Chrome, Razor, and Bob. We're the Midnight Riders."

Bob turned around so Franklin could see two
blood-red letters on the back of his jacket: MR.

"We couldn't fit the whole thing on the jackets," Wolverine explained. He took a step back
and examined Franklin from head to foot.
"You've made some interesting choices, Benjie."

"Choices? I . . . I beg your pardon?"

"Your clothing. Very intriguing. I think it
reflects your character. Solid, sturdy, and with
great spirit and integrity."

"Todd!" Mr. Snodgrass grumbled. "Have you
been sniffing your mother's cellulite cream
again?"

Ignoring his father, Wolverine said, "Very
distinctive. Old world with a modern flair."

"Y-you mean to say that you like my clothes?"
Franklin asked uncertainly.

"Yes. They are as much an expression as my jewelry and tattoos. And speaking of tattoos . . . you should get one on your scalp."

Fascinated by this strange fellow, Franklin stumbled through the conversation. All the while, he kept looking over at the motorcycles curiously. When Wolverine asked Franklin if he'd like a ride, Mr. Snodgrass blurted, "Absolutely not, Benjie, I'd feel responsible." He put a hand on Franklin's shoulder and turned to his son. "Benjie's a *guest,* Todd; how many times I gotta tell you I'm not gonna let you kill our guests? Go take your mother for a ride, or something."

But Franklin *wanted* a ride, and insisted on accepting Wolverine's invitation.

Now he sat with them inside the colorful and noisy TeenTech Club.

A pretty blond girl with pad and pen in hand hurried up to their table with an order pad and said, "Hi! What can I get for ya tonight?" Like everyone else in the club, she had to shout to be heard in all the noise.

Franklin asked Wolverine to order for him.

After the waitress had taken all the orders and hurried away, Bob said something to everyone at the table, gesturing with one hand, shaking his head as he grinned. But it was all gibberish and didn't make a bit of sense.

"Bob's our newest member," Wolverine said. "He just moved here from the Smoky Mountains. We can't understand a word he says, so we just nod a lot and he doesn't seem to mind."

"What is that *dreadful* sound?" Franklin asked.

"Oh, that's U2," Wolverine replied.

"Me, too?" Franklin asked.

"No. U2. The band. They're the ones making that music."

"Music?" Franklin blurted, unable to hide his shock. "That most certainly is *not* music! It sounds as if the whole world is falling in on itself!"

As they talked, Razor sat in his chair, motionless, his eyes covered by jet-black sunglasses. He looked like a mannequin.

The waitress brought their drinks, and Franklin sipped his. "This is *delicious!* What is it?"

"Razzleberry soda," Wolverine said.

Franklin finished his soda in no time and smacked his lips with pleasure. Then he sighed and said, "I should be getting back. My generous hostesses are quite likely wondering about me by now."

"No, no," Wolverine said. "You liked that razzleberry soda . . . lemme get you another." He waved the waitress down, ordered another soda for Franklin, then smiled at him and said, "You need to relax. Enjoy yourself. Don't be so uptight."

The waitress brought Franklin a second soda, and as he made his way to the bottom of the glass, a lovely young woman with half her head shaved danced over to his side. The other half of her head was covered with long, wavy red hair. She stood there and smiled down at Franklin, moving back and forth to the beat.

"Benjie," Wolverine said, nodding toward the young woman. "I think she wants you to dance with her."

When Franklin saw her, he stood immediately, saying, "Forgive my ill manners, madam. Benjamin Franklin at your service." He bowed and kissed her hand, then stood, smiling.

"Benjamin Franklin, huh?" the young woman said, still moving to the beat.

"That is right," Franklin said, frowning at the woman's odd movements.

"You're the guy who tied a key to a kite and then flew the kite in an electrical storm?" she asked, grinning.

"My *goodness!*" Franklin blurted. "People remember me for *that?*"

The young woman said, "Hmm, Benjamin Franklin. Nice to meet you. I'm Tanya."

"Tell me, Tanya," Franklin said, still frowning, "is there something wrong with you?"

"No. I just like to keep with the beat, that's all.'" She held out her right hand to him. "C'mon and dance with me, Benjamin Franklin!"

"Oh, I, er, uh . . . no, no, thank you, but I am afraid not, young lady." He turned to sit down again.

"Go ahead and dance with her, Benjie," Razor

said, speaking for the first time. "Have some fun."

"Well, I . . . I suppose," Franklin said reluctantly. But as he looked at the crowded dance floor, he couldn't conceal a smile at the thought of trying something so new, so *outrageous!* "All right, Tanya. We shall dance."

The Midnight Riders laughed happily as they watched Benjamin Franklin take to the dance floor of the TeenTech Club. And once he got started and found the beat . . . he really wasn't *bad!*

Sabrina and Salem went all the way around the house once before Mr. Snodgrass spotted them.

"You lookin' for Benjie?" he asked, startling Sabrina. He came around the front corner of his garage carrying a can of generic cola in one hand.

"Benjie? *Yes,* I'm looking for him," Sabrina said. "Have you seen him, Mr. Snodgrass?"

"Well, he was here a little while ago havin' a cola with me." He shook his head disapprovingly. "I told him not to go."

"Go *where?*"

"With my son. Benjie said he wanted a ride on Todd's motorcycle, so the five of 'em took off."

"Five?"

Mr. Snodgrass took a sip of his cola, belched, and nodded. "Yeah. My son, the other guys in his motorcycle gang, and Benjie."

Sabrina's mouth opened and closed a few times before any words came out: "Muh-muh-*motorcycle gang?*"

Scowling, Mr. Snodgrass said, "Yeah, the Midnight Riders. My son and his idiot friends goin' around dressed up like a bunch of MTV goofballs, or some dumb thing."

"Where did they *go?*" Sabrina asked.

He shrugged. "Who knows? Just graduated from high school and all he wants to do with his time is run around with his dippy motorcycle friends, lookin' like they're single-handedly keeping the leather industry in business, or somethin'."

"Don't you have any idea where they might be? Is there a place where your son and his friends hang out?"

He reached under his fishing cap and scratched his head. "Well, let's see . . . I've heard him talk about a place called the TeenTech Club, but I don't know where—"

"Thank you, Mr. Snodgrass!" She turned and started running toward the front door, with Salem keeping pace beside her. Sabrina stopped and turned back to Mr. Snodgrass. "If they come back with him, *please* don't let him out of your sight!" Then she ran into the house.

"What're we gonna do?" Salem asked once they were in the living room.

"I don't know, Salem, your guess is as good as mine." Sabrina began pacing. "If this situation is gonna get any worse, I wish it would do it now and get it over with, because the suspense is killing me."

"I say we get in the car and go look for him," Salem said. "He can't be *that* hard to find. We'll just look for four guys in black leather jackets on motorcycles with an old fat guy on the back of one."

"You're right, Salem. But first, I'm gonna go upstairs and see how—" She froze on her way to the stairs, then spun around, her eyes searching the room. "Where are Jenny and Harvey?"

Salem's ears tilted back and his fur stood on end for a moment as he quickly looked around the room. "Oh, no."

"They've gotta be here!" Sabrina said with a fearful quiver in her voice. "Jenny! Harvey! Where *are* you?"

They came out of the kitchen a moment later. Jenny held a jar of chocolate syrup from the cupboard in one of Harvey's hands and a spoon in the other, and there was chocolate on her lips.

"How come you guys don't have a refrigerator?" Harvey asked in Jenny's voice.

In Harvey's body, Jenny clenched her fists and stomped a foot as she cried, "Would you *please* tell him to *stop eating!* By the time he's done with me, I'm gonna look like a Winnebago with freckles!"

Sabrina sighed with relief when she saw them, but she ignored what they'd said and turned to the cat. "Salem, keep an eye on both of them while I go upstairs. Don't let them leave this *room!*" She hurried upstairs.

Salem took a few steps toward Jenny and Harvey, puffing himself up, looking stern and threatening. "Remember," he said, "I'm related to the king of beasts!" Then he growled.

Jenny and Harvey shuddered when Salem spoke to them, and they cried at the same time, *"Blegghh!"* They turned and ran back into the kitchen.

"Oh, funny," Salem said as he followed them. *"Verrry* funny."

In the kitchen, Harvey said with Jenny's voice, "See? I *told* you I heard the cat talk earlier! This is one *bizarre* dream!"

Chapter 10

I haven't seen Zelda," Aunt Hilda said to Sabrina, who stood beside her bed. "Either she can't find Drell, or he's so furious about the whole thing, he's sprouted horns, or tentacles, or something. I'm *so* worried."

"Well, we've got new problems, Aunt Hilda. I've lost Benjamin Franklin."

Aunt Hilda's eyes widened slowly. In the backyard, the cow mooed ominously. One of Aunt Hilda's hiccups made the bed rattle and creak.

"What do you *mean* you lost him?" she asked breathlessly. "How do you *lose* one of the fathers of our country? I mean, he's a little bigger than an earring or a contact lens!"

"I'm sorry, Aunt Hilda, but I had to go get Harvey. I mean, to get *Jenny.* And while I was gone . . ." Sabrina shrugged helplessly. "I told Salem to keep an eye on him, but there's only so much a cat can do."

"So, he wandered off on his own. Probably out looking for a party. He's a very squirrelly man, you know."

"He took off with a motorcycle gang and—" Sabrina was startled into silence when a woman appeared in the room in a flash of sparks.

"Hello," the woman said. "Which one of you is Hilda?"

The woman wore a white jumpsuit that almost looked like a medical uniform . . . except for the white sequins all over it. She was painfully thin and had a small head beneath her enormous helmet of bright green hair, and behind her large, oddly shaped glasses. Her broad smile revealed teeth bigger than Chiclets. She carried a black satchel with a yellow smiley face on the side; the smiley face wore a stethoscope.

Aunt Hilda raised a hand cautiously. "That would be me."

"Hello, Hilda. I'm Doctor Ronda Proctor." She laughed a loud, honking laugh. "Actually, I'm not a doctor *yet,* but I love saying that really fast. Doctor Ronda Proctor." She laughed again. "Anyhoo, I'm one of Dr. Leiderhosen's senior students, and I'm here in response to a call from—"

"Yes, yes, I know," Aunt Hilda said, frowning. "A *student!* Nothing personal, Proctor Ronda, but I—"

"Doctor Proctor," Ronda said. "Er, actually, Ronda Proctor, without the doctor, because I'm not a doctor yet. But I will be soon."

"Yes, that's the problem. I told Zelda I didn't want to *see* a student!"

"Well, yes, that's what she said," Ronda said, nodding. "But, look . . . it was either come here and check on you, or it was my turn to clean the bathroom in the doctor's lounge."

"Maybe you should at least let her examine you, Aunt Hilda," Sabrina said. "It couldn't hurt."

"Hey, let's not get her hopes too high, okay?" Ronda said. She put an arm around Sabrina and led her to do the door. "Why don't you step outside for just a second, and I'll take a look at your aunt."

Sabrina went out into the hall. Exactly one second after the bedroom door closed, it opened again and Ronda said, "Okay, we're done, you can come back in." Sabrina followed her back into the bedroom as she went on: "I honestly can't find anything wrong. She seems perfectly healthy to me. But I'd like to remind you that I'm *not* a doctor yet."

"Yes, we know," Sabrina said.

"Well, it's just that, sometimes, everybody gets caught up in all the medical excitement and they forget, so I was just reminding you."

"All *right,*" Sabrina said, rolling her eyes. "Now, what are we going to do about my aunt's hiccups?"

"Hiccups?" Ronda looked from Sabrina to Aunt Hilda, puzzled. "You have hiccups?"

"Oh, for *crying* out *loud*," Aunt Hilda complained. "You aren't a *student* . . . you're a jack—"

Aunt Hilda hiccupped.

Doctor Ronda Proctor, who was not yet a doctor, disappeared and was replaced by a braying donkey.

"Aunt *Hilda!*" Sabrina exclaimed in horror, gawking at the donkey.

"Oh, no! Oh, dear. I-I-I didn't muh-mean it, I . . . well, yes, I *meant* it, because she was *really* starting to get on my *nerves* . . . but I didn't mean for *this* to happen!" Aunt Hilda covered her face with both hands and groaned miserably.

Sabrina's heart pounded against her ribs so hard, she could feel it in her ears. She didn't know how much longer she would be able to put up with the unbearable suspense and unpredictable surprises of Aunt Hilda's hiccups.

"Where did this donkey come from?" Sabrina asked.

"Oh, *please,* Sabrina," Aunt Hilda said. "Do I look like the kind of person who knows where donkeys *come* from?"

Sabrina sighed. "Well, wherever she is . . . I hope Doctor Ronda Proctor is okay."

"She wasn't a *doctor*. She was a witch, though, so she'll be fine." Aunt Hilda sat up straight and looked serious. "What are we going to do about Benjie?"

"I'm going to have to go look for him," Sabrina replied. "And I'll have to take Jenny and Harvey with me so I don't make the same mistake *twice.*"

"Listen, sweetie," Aunt Hilda said with genuine concern, "why don't you go to the linen closet and track down Zelda?" She hiccuped so hard, she nearly fell over on the bed.

"That's why," Sabrina said. "Aunt Zelda's trying to find someone who can stop *that,* and I don't want to bother her. I already know where this motorcycle gang hangs out."

"All right, but . . . be careful."

"I will, Aunt Hilda," Sabrina said as she leaned down and kissed her aunt on the forehead. "And you try not to think, okay?" Sabrina left the bedroom but stopped in the hall, turned back silently to Aunt Hilda's door, and listened. When she heard nothing, she carefully peered around the doorjamb.

Aunt Hilda was lying in bed on her side, with her back to the door.

Sabrina got down on hands and knees and crawled through the door, across the bedroom, to the foot of Aunt Hilda's bed, where she hunkered a moment, listening.

Aunt Hilda's breathing was rhythmic and restful.

As Sabrina shot to her feet, she turned herself into Jerry Springer, with a microphone in hand.

"At what point," Jerry Springer asked, "did you realize that you had married your brother?"

Aunt Hilda rolled onto her back and began to flail her arms and legs as she screamed in horror.

And then she hiccupped.

Sabrina became herself again in a wink, and sighed. "I'm sorry, Aunt Hilda . . . I thought it was worth one more try."

"Oh, thank you, dear," Aunt Hilda said, smiling. "That's so sweet."

When Sabrina left the room again, she went downstairs.

In the kitchen, she found Jenny and Harvey eating like a couple of expectant mothers. Salem was curled up on the island watching them. When she walked in, Salem's eyes met hers, as if to say Jenny and Harvey were pathetic.

Jenny turned to Sabrina and, from inside, Harvey asked, "Why don't you have a refrigerator in here?"

"I'm sorry, Jenny, but our refrigerator turned into a cow."

"I'm not *Jenny!*" Jenny snapped. "I'm *Harvey.*"

"Yes, I'm sorry, Harvey, I've just got a lot on my mind right now and—"

"Would you *stop* worrying about a refrigerator?" Jenny barked from Harvey's body. "You're gonna turn me into a *bus* if you keep eating like this!"

"Oh, Harvey, would you forget about your weight for just a *second!*" Sabrina said.

"I'm not *Harvey!*" Harvey snapped. "I'm *Jenny!*"

"Okay, that's *it!*" Sabrina said, raising her arms. "Nobody speak. *Nobody* . . . but *me*. In fact, don't say another word until I *say* you can. Got it?"

Salem stretched out on the island and looked terribly uninterested.

Sabrina took a few deep, calming breaths, then said, "We're gonna have to leave now. I've got to find someone, and I don't have time to argue with you about whose name I should use. This is very confusing for all of us, but for the time being . . . just *don't speak*. Okay?"

Jenny and Harvey nodded their heads, but did not make a sound.

"If that was in any way directed at me," Salem said, "I'll start coughing up hairballs in your shoes."

"No, not you, Salem," Sabrina said. "I know who you are. Okay, you two," she said to Jenny and Harvey, "come with me."

"Hey, I'm coming, too!" Salem said, hopping down from the island.

"No, Salem, you'd better stay here with Aunt Hilda."

"With *those* hiccups? I can't get far *enough* away from her! And besides . . . I feel responsible for Benjie slipping out like that.

"Well," Sabrina said hesitantly, "I guess you can come, as long as you promise to stay in the car."

Together, they went through the living room and out the front door.

"Where are we going, anyway?" Salem asked. Sabrina said, "To the TeenTech Club."

As Sabrina and her friends were leaving the house, Wolverine was becoming impatient at the TeenTech Club. When the song that was playing came to an end, he stood and walked over to the edge of the dance floor.

"Okay, Benjie!" he called. "That was the last one."

Franklin elbowed his way through the crowd to Wolverine's side, holding Tanya's hand all the way. His face was glistening with perspiration, his spectacles were crooked, and his stringy hair was splayed in all directions. And he was grinning like a dizzy little boy.

"Oh, are you certain, Wolverine?" Franklin asked. "Won't you join us for one last dance? It's such *delightful* fun!" he said with a giggle.

"Well, you've been having delightful fun for about forty-five minutes now," Wolverine said, "and I'm afraid you're going to drop dead on us. Besides, I have an appointment to keep." He turned to Tanya and said, "You can come along, if you'd like."

Tanya's grin wasn't as enthusiastic as it had been earlier, and she was trying to catch her breath. "Yeah, Benjie, maybe you should go. I mean . . . you've worn me *out!*"

"You wanna come, too, Tanya?" Wolverine asked.

"Uh, well . . . yeah, sure, why not?" she sputtered breathlessly. "I'm not gonna be dancing anymore tonight, *that's* for sure!"

The six of them went outside to the motorcycles. Franklin rode with Wolverine again, and Tanya rode with Chrome.

"Where are we going?" Franklin asked.

"To see an artist."

"An artist?" Franklin asked excitedly. "How *wonderful.*"

"His name is Phlegm."

"Phlegm?" Franklin asked, frowning. "Well, is he a painter? A sculptor?"

"Tattoos. He's finishing up the two-headed snake on my back," Wolverine said as he fired up his hog.

☆

Chapter 11

☆

Sabrina parked the car beside the TeenTech Club, killed the engine, then turned to her friends. "Okay, listen," she said. "I don't see any motorcycles parked around here right now, but I'm gonna go inside anyway and ask around. Maybe somebody knows where to find the Midnight Riders. But while I'm gone—and I'm *serious*, now, okay? Are you listening?"

Jenny and Harvey nodded.

"Good. Because this is *very* important. While I'm gone, do . . . *not* . . . leave this car. Do you understand me?"

They nodded again.

"Salem," Sabrina went on, "you have my permission to scratch them both to shreds if they even *look* like they're thinking about getting out of the car, all right?"

"Oh, goody," Salem said flatly. "Once again, the responsibility is on my small feline shoulders." He rolled his eyes . . . an action that looked rather odd when it was performed by a cat.

"I'll be back in just a few minutes," Sabrina said as she opened the door. She left the car and went into the club.

When she first walked in the door, she stopped to let her eyes adjust to the darkness and her ears adjust to the thundering music. Deep inside the club, she saw the beams of laser light darting back and forth over the heads of the people on the dance floor.

"Can I help you?"

Sabrina turned to see a man standing behind a short, narrow counter. He was short and had thinning dark hair with plenty of gray in it. He spoke in a gravelly voice with a heavy New York accent. He was probably in his fifties and had a toothpick sticking out of his mouth.

"Uh, yes," Sabrina said. "I'm looking for somebody named Todd."

The man stared coldly at her for a moment. "What do I look like, the Missing Persons Department? There's a two-dollar cover. You wanna leave, I stamp your hand so you can come back, and dat's it. Anything else . . . I can't help ya."

Sabrina winced at his unfriendly tone. "Well, see, I understand he comes here a lot, and it's really important that I—"

"People named Todd don't come here," the man grumbled. "And people who come here ain't named Todd, if you know what I mean. And if you don't mind my sayin', sweetie, you give me the very distinct depression of a person who don't come here, if you know what I mean."

Sabrina's look of discomfort suddenly became one of annoyance. "My name is Sabrina . . . *not* Sweetie."

The man lifted his hands in a gesture of peace. "Hey, I'm sorry, okay? I mean, listen . . . forget about it."

"Look, this guy Todd is in a motorcycle gang called the Midnight Riders," Sabrina said.

A bushy eyebrow popped up over the man's eye and he smirked. "Oh, yeah. The MRs. You must be talkin' about Wolverine."

"Who?"

"Wolverine. The leader of the MRs. I'm guessin' you're talkin' about Wolverine, because I know Chrome, Razor, and Bob . . . and no girl as pretty as you is gonna come lookin' for *dem.*"

Sabrina was finding the man more annoying by the minute.

"Well, are they *here?*" she asked.

"They were. Left about ten minutes ago."

Sabrina gasped. "Do you know where they were going?"

The man's face soured as he said, "Kids like

that? Wearin' black leather and ridin' motorcycles? I don't even know where they *come* from,
let alone where they're goin'.'"

"Well, if you hate them so much, why don't
you work somewhere *else?*"

"Work?" the man blurted. "I've owned this
club for over twenty years, honey. It's been a
disco, a country and western club, a punk club,
and for about two weeks in 1995, it was a club
that played only John Tesh music, but nobody
bought any drinks, they just sat around *smilin'*
alla time, so I scrapped that idea. Now it's a club
for teenagers, no alcohol, no smokin', just loud
music and a lotta dancin'. I don't gotta like
people to take their money, if you know what I
mean."

The man made Sabrina squirm with discomfort. "So, you don't know of *any* place where
Wolfman—"

"Wolverine," the man interrupted. "And no, I
don't know where he hangs out. Don't wanna
know. Tell ya the truth, I don't wanna know
anybody who'd hang out *here.*"

"You hang out here," Sabrina said.

"Hey, I just *work* here, okay?"

Sabrina turned and headed out of the club
but she stopped at the door and looked back.
The man was shouting rudely at someone who
had spilled a drink a few yards away. A mischie-
vous smirk curled the corners of her mouth and
she waggled the fingers of one hand.

The owner of the club was suddenly decked

out in cowboy gear—hat, shirt, chaps, and cowboy boots with spurs—and the music playing in the club suddenly went from pounding techno-pop to loud country and western music. The owner looked down at his clothes and made a sound of sputtering confusion. Then he turned to the dance floor farther inside the club.

All movement on the dance floor stopped and a grumbling murmur quickly became an angry roar as everyone headed for the front of the club . . . for the owner.

"No, no, *wait!*" he cried, holding up his arms. "I-I-I don't know what huh-happened! I-i-it's a technical difficulty! That's all! Just . . . just . . . hey, *hey!* Just *back off!*"

Sabrina left the TeenTech Club, muffling her giggles behind a tight-lipped smile. Outside, she got in the car and started the engine.

"They left here about ten minutes ago," she said as she pulled away from the curb. "That means they couldn't have gotten too far."

"So, what do we do now?" Salem asked.

"We *look* for them," Sabrina replied. "Four motorcycles, four guys in black leather . . . and Benjamin Franklin. Shouldn't be *too* hard, should it?" She looked in the rearview mirror at her friends, and noticed an odd, pinched look on Jenny's face. "What's the matter?"

"I'm hungry," Jenny said.

"You are *such* a pig!" Harvey said. "Is there any time of the day when you *don't* eat? I mean, if I ate like you, I'd look like a *building!*"

"Could you two just calm *down?*" Sabrina pleaded. "We don't have any food, Jenny, so I can't—"

"I'm *Harvey!*" Jenny said.

"And don't forget," Harvey said, "I'm *Jenny!*"

Sabrina rolled her eyes and groaned. "My head's gonna explode, I just know it." She took a deep breath and let it out slowly, then glanced in the rearview mirror. "Okay, fine. One of you is Harvey and one of you is Jenny, and one of you is hungry, and one of you is having weight gain anxiety. But you *both* need to calm down and be quiet because I don't have time for that right now. And *besides* . . . this is a dream. So you're *not* really hungry, and nobody's gonna gain any *weight!* Okay?"

No one said anything. The car became terribly quiet.

"I said, *okay?*" Sabrina tried again.

Harvey and Jenny agreed quietly from the backseat.

Salem said, "This is just *so* much fun."

Chapter 12

☆

☆

The Midnight Riders roared down a narrow sidestreet in the darker part of town. They slowed to a stop in front of a shop with a blackened window and a neon sign that read:

PHLEGMWORLD
- Tattoos -
- Body Piercing -
- Hair Dyeing -
- Paintball Equipment -

They parked their motorcycles in front of the shop and went to the blackened glass door.

"Come meet Phlegm, Benjie," Wolverine said, holding the door open for Franklin.

Inside, there was plenty of light, but the black

walls made it *feel* dark. There was a rack of T-shirts, a rack of skirts, one wall covered with tattoo samples, a shelf of paintball equipment, and a gumball machine.

Behind the small counter in the back stood an enormously fat man with a completely bald head and a bushy black mustache the size of a guinea pig. He had a gold ring in his nose and wore a tentlike white T-shirt with a grinning Daffy Duck on the front. There was a coiled snake tattooed on the top of his otherwise shiny head. He was talking on the phone, but gave them a friendly wave.

"Phlegm's not his real name," Wolverine whispered, leaning toward Franklin. "He came here from Turkestan a couple years ago and only knew about three words of English. We always made fun of his bad English. He got a kick out of it, too, because he knew we meant no harm. Well, he decided he wanted an American name, something his American friends could *pronounce,* so we suggested Phlegm. But it kinda stuck . . . and we've never had the heart to tell him we were only joking."

"Wolverine, my good friend," Phlegm said, hanging up the phone. He had an Eastern European accent that was so heavy, his words were sometimes difficult to understand.

Wolverine made small talk with Phlegm for a moment, then introduced Franklin.

"Before you get to work on my two-headed snake, Phlegm," Wolverine said, "what do you think might be fitting for my friend Benjie from Philadelphia? A tattoo? A piercing?"

Phlegm frowned thoughtfully as he studied Franklin's face a moment. Then he grinned, his crooked teeth appearing beneath his giant mustache. "Why not *both!*"

Sabrina drove slowly through town, turning down side streets, doubling back as she drove around blocks. There was a heavy silence in the car that was beginning to make Sabrina feel even more uncomfortable than she did already.

"How are you two doing back there?" she asked, glancing in the rearview mirror.

"I'm fine," Harvey's voice said.

Jenny's voice, on the other hand, sounded a bit whiny. "Can't we hit a drive-through? I mean, it wouldn't take long, would it? Just a few minutes, right? I could really use a burger, or something. I haven't had dinner, and I'm—"

"You ate everything in Sabrina's *kitchen!*" Jenny said with Harvey's voice. "A whole jar of chocolate syrup? *That* was your dinner, okay? Remember, that's *my* body you're walking around in! How would you like it if, while I'm in *your* body, I got a tattoo, or shaved your head, or had all your gross, disgusting *teeth* removed?"

"Would you leave my teeth alone?" Harvey replied with Jenny's voice.

Exasperated, Sabrina said, "If you two don't

stop it right now, I'm gonna pull this car *over,* okay?"

They fell silent.

"Jenny's right," she went on, *"none* of us have eaten, and we're all—"

"I'm Harvey," Jenny said.

"Don't *start* that again!" Sabrina snapped. "There's a Burger Boy just up the block. I'll go to the drive-through. Everybody tell me what you want *now,* though, so we can save time once we get there."

"Get me a fish sandwich," Salem said.

"Not *you,"* Sabrina replied.

Harvey spoke from Jenny's body: "I'd like the double bacon cheeseburger with onion rings and a chocolate shake."

"No!" Jenny cried from Harvey's body. "Just get him a regular burger and *no* shake! A double bacon cheeseburger will go *straight* to my thighs."

Sabrina clutched the steering wheel so hard, her knuckles turned white, and said, "Maybe this was a stupid idea!" But she pulled into the Burger Boy parking lot anyway.

Hilda didn't like being alone. Even Salem at his whiniest or most snide was better company than no company at all. But it was even harder than usual now, because she couldn't allow herself to think about anything specific. The hiccups did not have the same regular rhythm that most *normal* hiccups had, so she never knew when one was going to hit. If she was thinking the wrong thing when it *did* hit, she could wreak more havoc. She didn't want that. So she recited the alphabet in her head, did the multiplication tables, anything to keep her mind occupied. Hilda was very relieved when her sister finally walked into the room . . . even though she had Drell with her.

"I hurried as fast as I could," Zelda said, "but Drell was in one of his solitary moods, so it took a while to find him."

"One of my *moods?*" Drell bellowed resentfully. "Need I remind you that I'm the head of the Witch Council? I don't appreciate being talked about so disrespectfully. And if I'm in a bad mood at *all,* it's because of what happened to all those people around the Maypole!"

"Oh, put a sock in it, Drell," Zelda said.

Drell was an enormous fellow, tall and imposing, with a booming voice. He was still wearing his festive red Beltane robe.

"What's going on?" Hilda asked. "Is Dr. Leiderhosen coming?"

"I got on the horn and left word for him to get here right away," Drell said. "I let him know that if he doesn't come, I will permanently ban him from the annual Witchcraft Open golf tournament."

Hilda said, "But isn't there some way to make me stop"—she hiccupped violently—"hiccuping?"

"Yes, Drell," Zelda said. "Every time she does that, something is happening *somewhere,* whether we notice it or not. The more she does it, the more—"

Suddenly, a figure appeared in the bedroom at the foot of Hilda's bed. It was short, and wore what appeared to be a purple wetsuit. It had enormous webbed flippers on its feet and wore an odd, seashell-like helmet with a black visor over the front, and a few hoses attached to a gelatinous object on its back. The figure carried in its right hand an object that looked like a cross between a golf club and a baseball bat.

The sudden appearance of this odd creature in the bedroom startled Zelda and Drell . . . but Hilda just smiled.

"Don't worry," she said. "It's just Sabrina trying to scare me again." She turned to the bizarre figure at the foot of the bed. "You might as well give it up, Sabrina," she said, hiccuping again. "It doesn't seem to be working."

The figure lifted the black visor on its helmet and a round, pink-cheeked face peered out at them with an expression of great irritation.

"My name is *not* Sabrina," the man said with a slight German accent. "I am Dr. Anton Leiderhosen! And I would like to know why I was called away from a conference at which *I* was the guest of honor!"

"You don't seem to be *dressed* for a conference," Zelda said.

"I was right in the middle of a game of Splooge!" Dr. Leiderhosen proclaimed heatedly. "And I was *winning!* I *never* win at Splooge, but this time I *was* winning . . . and my game was *interrupted!*"

"And I was the one who interrupted it," Drell said with great authority. "You're needed here, this is an emergency. Now . . . get out of that ridiculous outfit."

With a heavy sigh, Dr. Leiderhosen waved his arm and the strange costume was replaced by black pants, a white shirt, a gray tie, a long white doctor's coat, a stethoscope around his neck, and a black medical bag in his hand.

"My apologies, Drell," the doctor said, though his words sounded forced. "I was involved in my game, that is all. Now . . . what is the problem?"

Zelda told Dr. Leiderhosen about Hilda's hiccups, explaining all they knew about their effects.

"This is a serious condition," Dr. Leiderhosen said, going to Hilda's bedside.

"That's what *we* thought," Zelda said. "And it needs to be remedied immediately! And *then,* we have to send Benjamin Franklin back to 1776 Philadelphia."

The doctor turned to her with a look of horror. "The hiccups have dabbled with time and history?"

Zelda explained that Sabrina's library books

about Benjamin Franklin had changed places with the *real* Franklin, who'd been about to sign the Declaration of Independence at the Continental Congress.

"This is *disastrous!*" Dr. Leiderhosen cried. "If those books are read by anyone in 1776 Philadelphia . . ." He shuddered. "Where is Franklin now?"

"Benjie?" Zelda asked. "He's downstairs with Sabrina."

"No," Hilda said. "No, he's not. He's gone."

"Gone?" Zelda blurted. "Gone *where?*"

"I don't know," Hilda replied. "Sabrina went to look for him. With her friends Jenny and Harvey . . . who have switched bodies."

Dr. Leiderhosen slapped a hand to his forehead. "Insanity. This is pure *insanity!*"

"There's no way you're getting back to your game of Splooge," Drell said, "so don't act like this is too much for you."

"But this *is* insanity! I can cure the hiccups, and I can set right everything they have done. It is a serious condition, but not unheard of and not incurable. But if someone has been pulled out of the past and brought into the present . . . well, *that's* a different story altogether. I can send him back, and I can erase his memory of the experience . . . but he must be *here* in order for me to *do* it!"

Zelda looked down at her sister. "You don't know where they went?"

"Sabrina didn't know where Benjie had gone," Hilda said. "So . . . they could be anywhere."

There was a long, tense silence . . . then Drell said, "Leave it to you two to screw up American history."

Hilda and Zelda turned to him and said, simultaneously, "Put a sock in it, Drell."

After a long discussion about what would best suit Benjie, Phlegm grinned and spread his huge arms wide, saying, "Ah, then, we have decided?"

"Yes," Wolverine said. "An eagle tattoo on the top of his head, and a sparkly stud in his nose."

"Are you *certain* you can't do a turkey tattoo on my scalp?" Franklin asked Phlegm.

"I am *positive,*" Phlegm replied impatiently. "I told you, I don't *do* turkeys!"

"Look, Benjie," Wolverine said with a friendly smile. "As far as I'm concerned, you are cooler than cool already. The eagle and the nose stud will just add a little to your image."

"Cool, eh?" Franklin said with a boyish smile. "That's good?"

"Cool is *great,*" Chrome said.

Bob said something, too, and with great enthusiasm . . . but no one could make a bit of sense out of it.

"Go ahead and do Benjie's tattoo first, Phlegm," Wolverine said. "I can wait."

"No problem!" Phlegm cried, waving his

arms. "Oh! I almost forgot. I have a message for you, Wolverine." He reached beneath the counter and produced a white envelope. "It was delivered by a little boy this afternoon."

Wolverine opened the envelope, removed a slip of paper, and read the pencil-written block letters:

WOLVERINE—
BY THE TIME YOU READ THIS, WE
WILL ALREADY BE RIGHT BEHIND
YOU!!!
D&D

"Uh-oh," Wolverine muttered. "This is from the D&D . . . they're probably close, if they're not here already."

"The D&D?" Franklin asked.

"Yes," Wolverine said. "Another motorcycle gang. Our rivals. D&D . . . Dungeons and Dragons. That's all they do . . . play Dungeons and Dragons, and ride around on their hogs and make trouble."

"What can I do to help?" Phlegm asked.

"You just go ahead and do Benjie's tattoo, Phlegm," Wolverine said. "We'll keep an eye out for any trouble."

With that, Benjamin Franklin went into the back room with Phlegm to have an eagle tattooed on his bald scalp, and to have his nose pierced.

After he was gone, motorcycle engines roared outside. Wolverine, Chrome, Razor, and Bob all exchanged glances . . . although Razor's head never moved, and no one could see his eyes behind his dark glasses. Then, they headed for the door to go outside and meet their Dungeons and Dragons–playing rivals.

☆

Chapter 13

☆

I'm telling you," Salem said, "this is *not* a good neighborhood."

"How do *you* know?" Sabrina asked. "I mean, it's not like you know your way around town. You're a *cat!*"

"I'm an observant cat," Salem said. He gestured with his head as he said, "Over there, you got your abandoned bus station, and right next to it, you got your gun shop. Definitely a bad sign. And see that convenience store over there? Is it a chain store? A 7-Eleven? A Circle-K? No. The sign says Convenience Store. Need I say more?"

"Well, where *else* do you expect to find a motorcycle gang?" Sabrina asked, driving slowly as she turned down a side street. "In a *good* neighborhood?"

"Depends on the gang, I guess," Salem replied.

The car smelled of hamburgers and onion rings, and from inside Harvey's body, Jenny kept saying to her own body, in which Harvey resided, "I can't *believe* you actually ate that fat, greasy double bacon cheeseburger. I don't know how, but I'm gonna get *back* at you for that!"

Sabrina gasped suddenly. "Oh, look! *Motorcycles!*" she cried, pointing at a group of eight motorcycles parked in front of a small shop with a neon sign.

"Phlegmworld?" Salem asked, reading the sign. "Hey, I'm sorry, but that is just a little *too* disgusting for *me,* okay?"

On the sidewalk, two groups of four guys each were facing off, and the gathering looked hostile. One group wore baggy T-shirts, dark high-water slacks with cuffs, white socks, and black shoes; the other wore black leather, black jeans, and T-shirts.

"There they are!" Sabrina exclaimed. "The Midnight Riders! The ones in black leather! They're the ones Benjie ran off with!"

"Good grief," Salem muttered. "One of the fathers of our country has been kidnapped by morons with motorcycles!"

"But who are those *other* guys?" Sabrina asked as she pulled over to the curb.

"I don't know," Salem said, "but it looks like

the beginnings of a weirdo street brawl, if you ask me."

Sabrina turned off the engine and said, "Okay, everyone just sit tight. I'm gonna go see if I can find our guy."

She got out of the car and hurried toward the two groups.

"Hey, you guys!" she called. "Sorry to interrupt, but . . . I'm looking for a fat old man named Benjamin? Or maybe Benjie?"

The tallest of the black-leather group perked up. "You're looking for Benjie?" he asked. "I'm Wolverine."

"I've been looking for you!" Sabrina exclaimed. "Do you know where he is?"

"Yeah, he's in there," he said, waving toward the blackened glass door. "You know him?"

"Uh . . . yeah," Sabrina said. "Look, you guys, don't fight, okay? It's stupid, and it won't get you any dates." Then she hurried into Phlegmworld.

She spotted Franklin immediately; he was standing behind the small counter in the back chatting with an enormously fat man with a huge mustache. Franklin's head turned when he heard the door open, and he smiled when he saw her.

"Sabrina!" he called as he waved to her.

She hurried toward him, anxious to get him out of Phlegmworld and back to her house where he belonged . . . but she slowed down as she noticed something atop his head . . . not a hat . . . not a wig. . . .

It was a tattoo . . . of a large bird.

"What have you *done?*" she asked as she reached the counter.

"I have a tattoo!" Franklin said happily. He touched a finger to his nose and added, "And I have this! A sparkly stud in my nose!"

Sabrina made a high-pitched, scratchy noise in her throat, then leaned forward, put her elbows on the counter, her face in her hands, and groaned into her palms.

"Sabrina, my dear," Franklin said. "Have I done something to offend you?"

She stood up straight again and said, "No . . . it doesn't offend me. But I don't know how well the people back in Philadelphia are gonna take it."

"Well, young lady," Franklin said with a smile, "I'm not worried about *them* . . . so you should not worry either. My only regret is that Phlegm, here, does not do turkeys. I wanted a *turkey* on my head, but he insisted on an eagle."

"Get used to it," Sabrina said. "Now, let's go."

"What?" Franklin asked. "I must leave now?"

"I'm afraid so," Sabrina replied. "We have to go back to my place *immediately*. It's an emergency. And besides, if you don't leave now, you're probably gonna end up in a fight between motorcycle gangs."

"Er, uh . . . I beg your pardon?" Franklin asked.

"Never mind. Let's just *go!*"

And go they did.

Once outside, Franklin wanted to show Wolverine his new tattoo and nose-piercing, but Sabrina grabbed his arm and led him to the car. The two gangs were sitting on the curb, arguing over who'd had the most dates and talking about who could do the most damage to the other's faces. Sabrina decided not to ruin a good thing and just ignored them. When they were inside the car, Sabrina said, "Okay, we're all here, right?"

Everyone responded, even Salem, who was terribly annoyed because he had to share the passenger seat with Franklin.

"All right, fine," Sabrina said. She decided that driving back home would just waste time . . . so she waved a hand . . .

. . . and the car went from curbside in front of Phlegmworld to the driveway in front of Sabrina's house.

"Oh, that was cheating," Salem said.

Chapter 14

☆

☆

Sabrina rushed into Aunt Hilda's bedroom with Franklin, Jenny, Harvey, and Salem at her heels. Her hair was mussed and she was out of breath, but she smiled and said, "I found him!"

Aunt Hilda hiccuped.

"Oh, thank goodness!" Aunt Zelda exclaimed, clapping her hands together once. She quickly introduced Sabrina and the others to Dr. Leiderhosen, then blurted, *"Sabrina!* What have you *done* to Benjie?"

"I didn't do it, Aunt Zelda. He did it himself. The nose-piercing, too."

"Oh, that's just *great!"* Drell huffed. "How can we send Benjamin Franklin back to the Continental Congress with a tattoo on his head and a stud in his nose? They'll *never* understand. Those people don't even have *cable!*"

"There is nothing to worry about," Dr. Leiderhosen said. "The tattoo and stud would not be there if Hilda's hiccups had not pulled him into the future, therefore they are a result of the hiccups and will be reversed along with everything else."

Dr. Leiderhosen opened his bag and removed a shiny brass bowl and several vials of powders and liquids of various colors . . . blue, red, green, purple, and pink. He set the bowl in front of him, on absolutely nothing . . . it floated on air. With a wave of his hand, a flickering blue flame appeared beneath it. He poured the contents of the vials into the bowl, then twirled his finger in circles an inch above it, stirring the mixture. A thick, rainbowlike mist wafted over the edges of the bowl. When he was done, he waved his hand again and the flame disappeared. Then he took the bowl between both hands and stepped over to Hilda's bedside.

"Drink this," he said.

She frowned as she took the bowl in both hands. When she sniffed the thick, multicolored contents, her nose wrinkled and she said, "I will *not!*"

"Drink it!" Drell bellowed. "The man interrupted his Splooge game, for crying out loud! So go ahead and *drink* it!"

Sabrina watched as Aunt Hilda brought the edge of the bowl to her quivering lips, took a sip, then made a gagging sound.

"Don't sip it," Dr. Leiderhosen said, annoyed, "just drink it down!"

So she did. Her gulps were loud and her face looked disgusted, but she drank every last drop.

"Eewwww!" Aunt Hilda cried, shuddering as she shook her head back and forth. "That's even worse than Venusian mead!"

"Well, if you'd stayed away from the Venusian mead in the *first* place," Aunt Zelda said, "you wouldn't have to drink it, so it's your own fault, dear."

"Somebody give me something to get that taste out of my mouth!" Aunt Hilda said with an ill look on her face.

"No!" Dr. Leiderhosen snapped. "You must not drink or eat anything for an hour. Except this." He held out his hand, cupped it, and a fat, delicious-looking muffin appeared in his palm in a sparkly cloud. The top was covered with a shimmering glaze and sprinkled with odd-looking nuts. "The ingredients of this muffin will enable you to reverse everything your hiccups have done." He held it out to her. "Eat it."

Aunt Hilda took the muffin and bit into it, chewed for a moment . . . then her face screwed up in disgust. "This tastes like *sawdust!*" she blurted, mouth full, spraying muffin crumbs all over herself.

Everyone in the room shouted simultaneously, *"Eat it!"*

"Oh, this is just *cruel!*" Aunt Hilda complained. But she ate the muffin, frowning and gagging the whole time. When she was done, she said, "I'd better have something to eat and drink in an hour, or none of you are going to want to be in the same room with me . . . *got* it?"

"No problem, Hilda," Aunt Zelda said. "I'll have a *feast* ready for you in an hour if this works."

"Well," Aunt Hilda said, "it had *better* work, because if it doesn't I'm not going to—"

She was rocked by another seismic hiccup.

"Hey!" Aunt Hilda said to Dr. Leiderhosen. "I thought you were supposed to *cure* me of the hiccups!"

"And I have," the doctor said. "But you have a lot of errant spells to correct. You will continue to hiccup until you've done that. Each hiccup is reversing the damage done by all your hiccups *before* you ate that muffin."

"But . . . but . . ." Aunt Hilda glanced at the others, distraught. "That means I could be hiccupping for . . . well, for another *day!*"

"Perhaps," Dr. Leiderhosen said with a nod. "But when they stop, they won't come back."

She hiccuped again, then said, in a quiet, defeated voice, "Yes, Dr. Leiderhosen."

Sabrina turned to the doctor and asked, "How can we be *sure* the hiccups are fixing things when we aren't even sure of everything her hiccups *did?*"

Dr. Leiderhosen looked at her with an indignant glare. "Because they *will!* I attended witch doctor school for nearly four centuries, and I *say* the hiccups will fix everything. And I'm *always* right. In fact," he added, turning to Aunt Zelda, "you will see *exactly* how right I am when you get my bill."

"But . . . what about them," Sabrina asked, nodding toward Jenny and Harvey, who looked just as uncomfortable as they had all evening.

"Yes," Aunt Zelda said. "You see, they go to school with Sabrina, and they don't know about, um . . . about *us.* At least, they're not *supposed* to."

"Well," Dr. Leiderhosen said, "they should be in bed." He waved a hand at them as if he were swatting at a fly, and they disappeared. "Now they're in bed. Asleep. When they wake up in the morning, they'll have no memory of this whatsoever. They will think they had a perfectly normal evening."

"And what about Mr. Franklin?" Sabrina asked.

"Because he was brought from the past, he will be returned to the exact place he was when your aunt hiccupped, and at the exact *instant* in time that he was removed. So, there are no worries now. Everything is taken care of. I will send my bill. *Now,*" he said to Drell, "if it's all right with you, I would like to get back to my game of Splooge."

"Oh, all right," Drell said. "But if this doesn't work, you'll be hearing from me. And I'll probably have your license revoked."

Dr. Leiderhosen chuckled. "With all due respect, Drell . . . I've had more licenses revoked than you'll *ever* issue. Now, if you will all excuse me, I have a Splooge game to win!" He waved his arm extravagantly, and disappeared in a flash of blue light . . .

. . . as Aunt Hilda quaked with another hiccup.

"This is so unpleasant," Aunt Hilda said, "and so *embarrassing!* I swear, if word of this gets beyond these walls, I'll punish all of you. I don't know how, but I will, and when you least expect it. Maybe you'll all suddenly find yourselves trapped at a Slim Whitman concert, or something." She belched again. "I don't know what, but it'll be *ugly!*"

"Don't worry, Aunt Hilda," Sabrina said. "We're all going to keep it to ourselves."

"As long as you promise never to touch another *drop* of Venusian mead!" Aunt Zelda snapped. "Otherwise, I'll tell everyone we know."

Aunt Hilda hiccuped again; the cow in the

backyard mooed, and the donkey brayed loudly, as if she'd disturbed them.

A thought occurred to Sabrina: Benjamin Franklin would be disappearing soon, returned to 1776 Philadelphia . . . and she hadn't even *started* working on her paper yet. She clutched his arm and said, "Aunt Hilda, Aunt Zelda . . . say your good-byes now, because I've got to talk with Mr. Franklin for a while before he goes back."

The women told Franklin how good it was to see him again, and he bowed to each of them, kissing their hands.

"Okay," Sabrina said when they were finished. She took Franklin's hand and said, "Let's go downstairs. We don't have much time." She led him out of the bedroom and down the hall.

For nearly two hours, Sabrina and Franklin sat at the kitchen table over tea. Sabrina listened and took notes in her notebook as Franklin talked. He told her about his childhood, about his love of England but his inability to tolerate the politics, and of his excitement about having a hand in the birth of a new country. He told her about the Continental Congress, from which he'd come that afternoon, and about the disagreements and arguments that had to be settled before everyone would agree to sign the Declaration of Independence.

Sabrina took pages and pages of notes, writing

as quickly as she could, and smiling as Franklin peppered his stories with jokes and anecdotes. And then, right in the middle of a sentence, Benjamin Franklin disappeared. Neatly stacked on the chair in which he'd been sitting were Sabrina's library books.

☆

Chapter 15

☆

Sabrina and Jenny met in front of the school the next morning and headed inside together.

"So, are you still not speaking to Harvey?" Sabrina asked.

"Well . . . I've been thinking about that," Jenny replied, frowning. "I had a dream last night."

"Oh? What kind of dream?"

"That's the problem. I don't remember. But it had something to do with Harvey and me. And whatever happened in the dream . . . well, it made me realize that maybe I was being a little too hard on Harvey. I mean . . . he seems to think Libby's okay. That doesn't say much for his intelligence, but then, Libby's nice to him because he's a jock, and Libby's a cheerleader and really popular and pretty and . . . well, Harvey's a *guy*, right?"

"Right," Sabrina agreed with a big, relieved smile. She didn't know if Jenny had actually had a dream the night before, or if her experience in Harvey's body had had the smallest sliver of effect on her . . . but as long as Jenny was no longer planning to cut herself off from Harvey, Sabrina didn't care.

"Of course," Jenny said, "I still feel the same way about Libby. I think she's a *witch.*"

Sabrina flinched and stumbled slightly when she heard the word. "A *witch?*"

"Yep. Only without the broom and pointy hat."

Inside the building, they met up with Harvey in the hall.

"Hey, you two," he said, smiling at them as he closed his locker. "Did either of you get anywhere with the American History paper?"

"No," Jenny said, frowning. "I meant to, but . . . I guess I just never got around to it."

"Yeah," Harvey said, nodding. "Me, too. I planned to get started last night, but before I knew it . . . well, the day was over and I was waking up to another one." He turned to Sabrina. "How about you? Make any progress?"

Sabrina shrugged, lifting her eyebrows high. "Oh, I, um . . . I made some notes, but that's all."

"I guess we'll just have to work harder tonight," Jenny said as they started down the hall together.

As they passed the rest rooms, Harvey said, "Hang on just a sec, I'll be right back." He hurried toward the rest rooms . . .

. . . and walked into the ladies' room.

Sabrina and Jenny gasped simultaneously as a couple of screams sounded from within the rest room. The door burst open and several girls rushed out into the hall looking shocked and angry.

A moment later, Harvey stumbled out, eyes wide. He looked stunned as he turned to Sabrina and Jenny.

"How did I make *that* mistake?" he blurted.

The girls shrugged.

Scratching his head, Harvey turned and went into the *appropriate* rest room.

"What do you expect from someone who thinks Libby's a nice girl?" Jenny asked, shaking her head pitifully.

Sabrina laughed. But once she started, she found it was hard to *stop* laughing. It was a giddy sort of laughter, filled with relief . . . because she was pretty confident that her experiences with historical figures and body-switching and cows in the kitchen were over.

She just hoped that, from now on, her aunts would stay healthy.

About the Author

Joseph Locke is the author of ten previous novels for young readers, including *Kiss of Death* and *Game Over*. He lives with his wife, Logan, and their dog, Tucker, in northern California.

What would *you* do with Sabrina's magic powers?

You could win a visit to the set, a $1000 savings bond and other magical prizes!

GRAND PRIZE
A tour of the set of "Sabrina, The Teenage Witch" and a savings bond worth $1000 upon maturity

25 FIRST PRIZES
Sabrina's Cauldron filled with one Sabrina, The Teenage Witch CD-ROM, one set of eight Archway Paperbacks, one set of three Simon & Schuster Children's books, and one Hasbro Sabrina fashion doll

50 SECOND PRIZES
One Sabrina, The Teenage Witch CD-ROM

100 THIRD PRIZES
One Hasbro Sabrina fashion doll

250 FOURTH PRIZES
A one-year subscription of Sabrina, The Teenage Witch comic books, published by Archie Comics

Name_____

Address_____

City_____State_____Zip_____

Phone(_____)_____

1432 (1of2)

Sabrina, The Teenage Witch™ Sweepstakes Official Rules:

1. No Purchase Necessary. Enter by mailing the completed Official Entry Form or by mailing on a 3" x 5" card your name, address and daytime telephone number to Pocket Books/Sabrina, The Teenage Witch Sweepstakes, 13th Floor, 1230 Avenue of the Americas, NY, NY 10020. Entries must be received by 7/1/98. Not responsible for lost, late, damaged, stolen, illegible, mutilated, incomplete, not delivered entries or for typographical errors in the entry form or rules. Entries are void if they are in whole or in part illegible, incomplete or damaged. Enter as often as you wish, but each entry must be mailed separately. Winners will be selected at random from all eligible entries received in a drawing to be held on or about 7/7/98. Winners will be notified by mail.

2. Prizes: One Grand Prize: A weekend (four days/three nights) trip to Los Angeles for two people (the winning minor and one parent or legal guardian) including round-trip coach airfare from the major airport nearest the winner's residence, ground transportation or car rental, meals, three nights in a hotel (one room, occupancy for two) and a tour of the set of "Sabrina, The Teenage Witch" (approximate retail value $3500.00) and a savings bond worth $1000 ($US) upon maturity in 18 years. Travel accommodations are subject to availability; certain restrictions apply. 10 First Prizes: Sabrina's Cauldron filled with one CD-ROM (a Windows 95 compatible program), one set of eight Sabrina, The Teenage Witch books published by Archway Paperbacks, one set of three Simon & Schuster Children's books and one Hasbro Sabrina fashion doll (approximate retail value $100). 25 Second Prizes: Sabrina, The Teenage Witch CD-ROM published by Simon & Schuster Interactive (approximate retail value $30). 50 Third Prizes: Sabrina doll (approximate retail value $17.99). 100 Fourth Prizes: a one-year subscription of Sabrina, The Teenage Witch comic books published by Archie Comics (approximate retail value $15). The Grand Prize must be taken on the dates specified by sponsors.

3. The sweepstakes is open to legal residents of the U.S. and Canada (excluding Quebec). Prizes will be awarded to the winner's parent or legal guardian if under 18. Any minor taking a Grand Prize trip must be accompanied by a parent or legal guardian. Void in Puerto Rico and wherever prohibited or restricted by law. All federal, state and local laws apply. Employees of Viacom International, Inc., their families living in the same household, and its subsidiaries and their affiliates and their respective agencies and participating retailers are not eligible.

4. One prize per person or household. Prizes are not transferable and may not be substituted except by sponsors, in event of unavailability, in which case a prize of equal or greater value will be awarded. All prizes will be awarded. The odds of winning a prize depend upon the number of eligible entries received.

5. If a winner is a Canadian resident, then he/she must correctly answer a skill-based question administered by mail.

6. All expenses on receipt and use of prize including federal, state and local taxes are the sole responsibility of the winners. Winners may be required to execute and return an Affidavit of Eligibility and Release and all other legal documents which the sweepstakes sponsor may require (including a W-9 tax form) within 15 days of attempted notification or an alternate winner will be selected. Winner's travel companions will be required to execute a liability release prior to ticketing.

7. By accepting a prize, winners or winners' parents on winners' behalf agree to allow use of their names, photographs, likenesses, and entries for any advertising, promotion and publicity purposes without further compensation to or permission from the entrants, except where prohibited by law.

8. By participating in this sweepstakes, entrants agree to be bound by these rules and the decisions of the judges and sweepstakes sponsors, which are final in all matters relating to the sweepstakes.

9. The sweepstakes sponsors shall have no liability for any injury, loss or damage of any kind arising out of participation in this sweepstakes or the acceptance or use of the prize.

10. For a list of major prize winners, (available after 7/15/98) send a stamped, self-addressed envelope to Prize Winners, Pocket Books/Sabrina, The Teenage Witch Sweepstakes, 13th Floor, 1230 Avenue of the Americas, NY, NY 10020.